Alison, Who Went Away

Alison,
Who Went Away

Vivian Vande Velde

Houghton Mifflin Company
Boston 2001

Copyright © 2001 by Vande Velde, Vivian

All rights reserved. For information about permission to reproduce
selections from this book, write to Permissions, Houghton Mifflin
Company, 215 Park Avenue South, New York, New York 10003.

www.houghtonmifflinbooks.com

The text of this book is set in 12-point AGaramond.

Library of Congress Cataloging-in-Publication Data

Vande Velde, Vivian.
Alison, who went away / Vivian Vande Velde.
p.   cm.
Summary: Three years after the disappearance of her older sister,
fourteen-year-old Sibyl and her family struggle to continue their
lives, separately and together.
ISBN 0-618-04585-6
[1. Missing persons—Fiction.   2. Sisters—Fiction.   3. Family
problems—Fiction.   4. Gay fathers—Fiction.   5. High school—
Fiction.   6. Schools—Fiction.]   I. Title.
PZ7.V377   My   2001   [Fic]—dc21   00-032032

Manufactured in the United States of America
HAD   10   9   8   7   6   5   4   3   2   1

To Jennifer and to Michael,
who shared their stories

Alison, Who Went Away

1

There are three of us—well, actually five, if you count my parents. No, wait, actually six, if you count both my father and my stepfather. But I'm not—what I'm saying is there are three *kids,* not three people, in the family.

There's my sister Alison, who moved away from home and who celebrated her nineteenth birthday—or didn't—without contacting us, and—I know, I know—nineteen is hardly a kid anymore, but I'm doing the counting, so I can count however I want.

I'm Sibyl—well, actually, Susan, but what kind of name is Susan for anybody who's younger than about forty-seven? I'm fourteen, which is a long way from forty-seven. Thank God.

Then there's my brother Bryan, who's five, which also is a long way from fourteen. Five from fourteen means I was nine when my mother and Wally were going about conceiving him, which was practically old enough for me to know what they were doing when they were doing it. I mean, you'd think parents would show a little self-restraint.

Not only that, but Bryan still wets his bed. No, wait, what I *should* say is he's started wetting his bed again, which for the most part I'd say is his own business, except that now he has to take a bath every morning. This means either I have to get up at something like five o'clock in the morning, or I have to keep banging on the door because Bryan takes these half-hour *soaks,* with the water constantly running, no less, so the poor little dear doesn't get chilled, and I have to keep reminding him that there's only a finite amount of water in the Western Hemisphere. And then when he finally *does* get out of the bathroom, leaving steamy mirrors and sodden towels behind, and I'm trying to take this lukewarm little shower, he invariably flushes the toilet in the powder room downstairs and my water practically turns off. I mean, how much pee is in the guy? You'd think he'd have lost it all at night.

Wally and Dad both say I could avoid the whole problem by taking my shower at night, which is about the only thing in the whole world they agree on, and which just goes to show how little men know about hair.

Mom says I should get up first—which, like I said, means during the dead of night—then she says I should be more tolerant of Bryan—he's having a hard time adjusting. I tell her I thought that's what we were paying the psychologist for. She says, real casual, like she's just thought of it, "Oh, yeah, speaking of the psychologist, he says it might be a good idea for you to come in, too."

"I don't wet my bed," I tell her.

"As a matter of fact, he thinks we should all come in, as a family."

"Yeah?" I say. "Should I be feeling your sheets?"

Maybe she thinks I mean this in a Sexual way. According to Mom, this generation is way too caught up in Sexual things—like the way we dress, the music we listen to, and how I get the dirty jokes on TV before she does. She gives me this tight little look she has when she thinks I'm trying to get away with something, but just then the bus beeps its horn and I get to yell, "Gotta go."

"Did you have breakfast?" she asks as I fumble with the new dead bolt on the door. Well, it's not really new—you'd think after a year and a half I'd have caught the hang of it. She knows I haven't had breakfast; I've only just this minute finished my hair.

"No time," I tell her, but she's already heading toward the kitchen.

"At least take an apple with you," she calls back.

"OK," I call, finally getting the door open and running across the front yard. I know her tricks. She's trying to fatten me up so no boy in his right mind would look at me. She thinks this will keep me safe. It worked for a couple months after Alison left, when I was depressed: "Here, Susan, have a doughnut. Here, Susan, ice cream will make you feel better."

Until I noticed my thighs were getting as big around as Arnold Schwarzenegger's.

Like wearing glasses isn't already enough to get me crossed off the lists of half the boys in the world.

Mom, of course, doesn't see it. Mom says I have a cute little figure.

Mom doesn't know what she's talking about.

2

Nothing's the same since Alison went away.

I go to Mother of Sorrows, one of Port Champlain's all-girls Catholic high schools. You'd think they'd be illegal under some sort of equal rights law, but for some reason they're not.

My family isn't even Catholic—we're Lutherans, and for that matter, we're pretty much Christmas and Easter Lutherans.

But after Alison moved out, my parents decided that Abe Lincoln High, where she'd gone, wasn't good enough for me. They decided that Mother of Sorrows was safer and more structured—just generally a better environment. I ask you: What kind of environment is a place with a name like "Mother of Sorrows"? Can you imagine the type of people who would sit around saying: "Gee, we're going to have a bunch of impressionable young girls spending four years of their lives here—what should we call the place? I know: something nice and uplifting—how about 'Mother of Sorrows'?"

No wonder half the kids here are depressed.

The only good thing I can say about Mother of Sorrows is that hardly any of the kids from my grammar school come here, so at least I don't get compared to Alison.

The place used to be staffed entirely by nuns. Now there aren't enough to go around, so fewer than half the teachers are nuns. We even have some male teachers. I ask you: What sense is that? No boys allowed, but men are?

Only a couple of the really old nuns wear the black outfits and veils like they do on TV and in the movies. I guess they figure when they're that old, it doesn't make any difference what they wear anyway. But you can always pick out the nuns, uniform or not, because they never learned how to dress or do anything with their hair.

The girls don't have uniforms; we have a dress code, which is even worse than uniforms because the only clothes that fit the code are so ugly you wouldn't be caught dead in them otherwise. People see you walking to and from the bus, and for all they know you *chose* to dress in a white, collared blouse and a black or navy blue skirt. (They added green this year, but the shades they allow are even worse than black or blue.)

My homeroom teacher is Mr. Rosenblum—a nice, traditional Catholic name. I figure he must be an ex-priest despite the name, based on the way *he* dresses. Mr. Rosenblum is a global studies teacher, and he has this current events board; every day we're supposed to put articles of interest on it. Like *anybody* in the class besides Rosenblum is interested.

This week, I'm part of the team responsible for the current events board, along with Wakisha Carsonne, Mary Amber DeFranco, and Carolyn Tumia. Friday, when Mr. Rosenblum called out our names, Wakisha, Mary Amber, and I—who sit right near each other because we're at the beginning of the alphabet—put our heads together and decided that it would be easiest to remember if we were each responsible for one area for the entire week. Wakisha said she'd bring in something in world news, Mary Amber volunteered for national, I said I'd do local. By the time Carolyn, who's the last person alphabetically, crossed the room, all that was left was sports.

So this morning, Carolyn's still grumbling, but she's got an article about the New York Giants cutting some tight end or rear end or whatever they're called, and Wakisha—who's a real suck-up—has a two-page article on somebody in the Middle East blowing up somebody else, and I'm smoothing out the article I brought, which is about a car accident on the expressway where they needed to cut off the roof of the car to get the bodies out. The next thing we know Mary Amber is standing next to us at the current events board, hissing that she forgot to bring something—do we have anything she can use?

Luckily I don't have to go through the ethical self-questioning of would-I-give-her-something-if-I-had-something-to-give-her? because all I have is the picture and one column of text, which is only about five inches long. Mary Amber is not one of my favorite people anyhow.

I tell her, with a clear conscience, "Sorry," but she grabs the article out of my hand and flips it over to the back. Nothing there but the obituaries, and luckily she didn't rip it.

"Who's got world news?" Mary Amber demands.

Wakisha throws herself backwards against the current events board, her arms outstretched to protect her article, which she's just finished stapling up there.

"What's yours?" Mary Amber asks Carolyn, who's seen what happened with me and says, "Football on this side"—she turns the paper over—"an ad for a muffler repair shop on this side."

We all look at Wakisha again.

"C'mon," Mary Amber wheedles. "You've practically got the whole A section there." Wakisha hesitates, and Mary Amber says, "If Mr. Rosenblum gets mad at me, he's likely to take it out on all of us."

It *is* a possibility.

Wakisha steps away from the board, and Mary Amber pries the staples loose with her fingernails, which are painted white. I think she looks like she's just finished a particularly sloppy job involving correction fluid, but Mary Amber is not the type to ask for fashion tips from somebody like me. She gets one of the pages loose and turns it over. "Can I take this?" she asks, already folding the section over and creasing it with her white nails. "Your article's so long—nobody will miss this little bit."

Wakisha doesn't look happy about it but she says, "OK."

Carolyn asks, "What did you find?"

Mary Amber uses the chalk tray to rip a straight edge. "There's going to be some program on TV tonight about Robert Deitz."

I shiver—me, the one with the picture of the car that needed a can opener to see who'd died in it. "That's local," I inform her.

"The guy who killed all those women?" Carolyn asks.

"No, the rock star," I say.

Mary Amber looks at the scrap of paper she's torn from Wakisha's article, like maybe she isn't sure. She pretends she's just checking to make sure the edge looks even. "If it's on network TV, it's national news," she says.

Mr. Rosenblum breezes into the room about two seconds before the bell rings for our first class. *I'm* just stapling my article up, because after Mary Amber finally adjusted hers to perfection, and Wakisha fixed up hers, and Carolyn grabbed the stapler and did hers, the stapler ran out of staples and I had to figure out how to get the thing reloaded. "Waiting until the last minute, are we, Miss Casselman?" Rosenblum asks. Sister Carlotta, the principal, has told everyone my name is Susan, and most of the teachers refuse to call me Sibyl, but Rosenblum is the only one who calls us "Miss."

He studies the current events board as the rest of the girls file out of the room. "Good, good," he says, passing Wakisha's and Carolyn's. "Grim—but OK," he tells me. "Be on time tomorrow." Sure, he thinks *I'm* the one who mooched my article from someone else.

9

Mary Amber sees him looking at her contribution to the board and says, "The article's about the TV show, not the killings."

"I can see that," Rosenblum says, refusing to be rushed, regardless of how far we have to run for our next class. He gives a wobbly hand gesture like he's not quite sure. "Borderline, Miss DeFranco," he finally decides. "But acceptable." He waves us out the door.

School: it's so fun and exciting I could puke.

3

First period is religion, which isn't as bad as it sounds because it's really women's health issues.

Next comes math, which is my best subject this year. I've discovered that if I take it slowly, logically, one step at a time, it isn't so bad. I've made this discovery because otherwise Miss Beckwith leans across my desk and asks if I need any help, and Miss Beckwith has notoriously bad breath.

In English, we're studying *Great Expectations*—need I say more?

For foreign language I'm taking Italian, because my family heritage is mostly German, and French and Spanish seemed too potentially useful. I was seriously considering Latin—it *is,* after all, a dead language—but my stepfather Wally said that could prove helpful since so many English words have a Latin origin. So I switched to Italian.

Next comes earth science. We've been doing a unit on weather systems, and last Friday we had a chart due: one week of comparing the weather forecast in the morning with the actual weather as reported in the evening. I made my chart on Friday during the last ten minutes of Italian. I wrote "Gray and dismal" for every day. "Occasional drizzles. Unseasonably depressing." I didn't need a newspaper for that. I didn't even need to leave the house for that.

Today Sister Beatrice hands back our charts, and I've gotten a C: points deducted for effort, but she can't quibble with my accuracy.

Naturally, lunch is the high point of my day.

In the cafeteria, my best friend Connie Miraglia sits down next to me, so excited she can barely keep her tray steady long enough not to dump everything on my back. Connie is my best friend from grammar school; this year lunch is about the only time I see her except in the hallways.

"Guess what," she says.

I don't even know where to start, so I just shrug. The other girls at the table know Connie, too. They know Connie doesn't demand guesses, but she *does* insist on some sort of verbal response. My brother Bryan went through a stage like this a couple years ago: "Guess what, Susan." "What, Bryan?"

Now Connie is going through that same stage. "Guess what," she repeats.

"What?" asks somebody who has more energy than I do.

"I just overheard Sister Carlotta talking to Mrs. MacNeely: There's going to be a dance—just for the freshman class—the last day of school before Christmas break."

Wakisha giggles. "Doesn't sound like much fun if it's *just* for the freshman class," she points out. "I'm willing to dance a couple fast ones with Sibyl, but there's no way I'm slow dancing with her."

"What makes you think I'd ask you?" I say, while Connie figures it out.

She rolls her eyes at how juvenile Wakisha and I are. "We get to invite boys," she explains. "That's the whole point." Lately, with Connie, that's *always* the whole point. "It's a special treat for us because we sold so much more chocolate than anybody else."

Easy for her to say. Connie has about three hundred relatives, none of whom, apparently, has a problem with weight or diabetes.

I only sold one box, and that was because I bought a candy bar for myself, and then when I brought back the rest, Mr. Rosenblum said no partial boxes. He says that was announced at the beginning, and everybody else seemed to know, but I think it's just a plot against the Lutheran kid. I had to buy up thirty-five chocolate bars at a dollar apiece, which used up the money I'd been saving for a certain black leather jacket that my mother refuses to buy for me. She says I'm too young for a black leather jacket, and I know better than to point out that Alison had one by the time she was my age. But maybe the psychologist has told Mom it's OK for me to make *some* choices in my life, because she's agreed I can have the jacket if I save up for it myself. Mom thinks I'm too easily distracted for that to ever happen.

Anyway, she and Wally wouldn't help me out with the

chocolate, even though other kids' parents brought boxes to work. Mom said it was about time I learned to be responsible for myself, and if I wanted my money back, I could always sell the chocolate from door to door in our neighborhood.

I'm teaching them, though. I've left the box on the kitchen counter with a sign saying $2.00 EACH. Mom, of course, has always had a lot of self-control. But so far I've sold three chocolate bars to Wally in one week. By the time I'm through learning to be responsible for myself, I should have enough money for that jacket.

Anyway, Connie's news about our chocolate-sale-celebration dance is about as exciting to me as the prospect of peddling chocolate to the neighbors. Everybody else at the table starts talking about what they're going to wear, even though Christmas vacation is more than two months away.

"Who're you going to invite?" Sharon Rescher-Smith asks me.

"Hard to say," I answer. "There're so many boys dying to take me out, maybe I'll need to organize a lottery to choose one."

"Oh, Susan, you're such a hoot," Sharon says.

While I debate which is more important, reminding her to call me Sibyl or laughing at her for using what's obviously one of her mother's thirty-year-old expressions, Connie says, "Come with me to the bathroom, Sibyl?"

Her timing is subtle enough that everyone guesses she doesn't really need to go, but wants to talk to me alone. So, nobody volunteers to come with us; instead, Wakisha presumes we're not coming back and commandeers my lunch, and the rest of the girls launch into Sharon, going "Hoot! Hoot!" so that they sound like a collection of shrill tugboats.

I follow Connie out of the cafeteria. Obviously, she has not been fooled by my talk of a lottery. Connie *knows* I need help.

4

In the bathroom, Connie—who's always assured me that my date for the eighth-grade formal wasn't all that bad—reveals her true thoughts. Without my saying a word about spilled punch, bruised toes, sweaty palms that wrinkled the back of my dress, or the kind of fourteen-year-old who has ambitions to be a professional bowler when he grows up, she tells me, "No more Freddie Dorfmeisters. It's time for you to meet boys on your own."

"Oh, it's time, is it?" I say. "Today? You're thinking I should start *now*? What do you think I've been trying to do since the summer between sixth grade and seventh, when you talked me into joining that stupid soccer team and Danny Stanford kicked the ball into my face and broke my glasses in the first five minutes of the first practice, and that was the best day I had?"

"Oh, Sibyl!" Connie says. "That isn't the point at all. The point is that you're not going about this the right way."

Connie, of course, never has to go about it at all. Prospective boyfriends seem to drop out of the trees whenever she walks by.

She asks me, "How are you going to meet anybody interesting if you spend all your time at Mother of Sorrows?"

"You're right," I tell her. "I'll cut classes tomorrow and hang around downtown watching all the drunks and bag ladies and Lincoln High dropouts. Someone fascinating is sure to engage me in meaningful conversation eventually."

Connie, who's known me just this side of forever and knows when I'm being sarcastic and when I'm being serious in a sarcastic tone, says, "Not amusing, Sibyl."

Two juniors come in to use the facilities. Connie has been checking herself out in the mirror and has assured herself that she looks presentable. Actually, she looks perfect. I don't even bother to check my own reflection, though I do check my glasses and finally realize that I'm not going blind, it's just that my lenses are all fingerprinty. I'm hoping Connie won't continue the conversation while the other girls are in here. She hikes herself up on the windowsill, which leaves me with the options of sitting down on one of the toilets or on the heat register, or of standing. Sitting on the register seems risky for mid-October. Those things can heat up *real* fast. I choose to stand.

"What I'm talking about, Sibyl," Connie says, even though the other girls are still here, "is a change of scenery."

"Yeah?" I say noncommittally, so the other girls won't know what we're talking about.

"How about spending some of your time at O'Gorman?"

This is a real letdown. Not only that, but one of the girls, who's washing her hands, gives me a wary look out of the corner of her eye. "Cardinal O'Gorman High School only accepts boys," I remind Connie.

Connie wiggles her eyebrows at me. "Exactly."

"Exactly?" I repeat. "Connie, I don't get your point."

"I'm talking about after school," Connie says. "Don't you read our own newspaper?" She pulls out a scrap of paper she's torn from last week's issue of the *Gabriel*. She's one of the staff writers, which is the only reason *she* reads it. "See, tonight's the last night of tryouts for their school play."

The two juniors are leaving the room. Before the door swings shut, I hear one sneering to the other, ". . . looking for boys."

I'm assuming they can figure out which one of us is more likely to find one.

Connie says, "Don't wrinkle your nose at me. It's a good idea."

I shrug. "Yeah, except for the fact that I can't sing, I can't dance, and I can't act."

"Neither can I," Connie assures me. "We'll sign up for the stage crew." She leans closer. "*Think* of all the boys that'll be there. And not just the theatrical types—there'll be basketball players wandering around, too, peeking into the auditorium between innings."

"Innings," I mutter to myself. "And all the troublemakers who've racked up detention points."

But it *does* sound interesting.

I shake my head. "My parents will never let me," I say.

"Why not?"

"Go out at night? By myself?"

"Most of the rehearsals are right after school. Only the try-outs and the dress rehearsal are at night." She sees I'm not convinced. "It's only—what?—about a ten-minute walk from here to there. And my mother would pick us up afterwards. What could happen?"

"You don't know how crazy my family's been lately," I tell her.

Though she does, because she's known *all* of us just this side of forever.

"I know how crazy you've always been," she counters.

"Which has nothing to do with anything," I tell her. "I'm lucky my mother has to work, or she'd be home-schooling me. That's how protective she's been since Alison moved out."

"I'll have my mother talk to her," Connie says.

It's a possibility, I suppose.

I nod, just as the first bell rings. We've been talking in the bathroom in the basement, behind the cafeteria. My next class is music, on the fourth floor, and I haven't been to my locker yet to pick up what I'll need for the afternoon.

Fifteen minutes in the john, and I go running out of there without even having had the time to pee.

5

After lunch, depending on the day, I have music, science lab, or phys. ed. Today it's music.

The nicest thing I can say about music is that it isn't science lab, and the nicest thing I can say about science lab is that it isn't phys. ed. I can't say anything nice at all about phys. ed.

After music is global studies. We spend the first few minutes of each class discussing the articles on that day's current events board. Mr. Rosenblum tells me that he asked the students in each of his earlier global studies classes who they thought brought in the picture of the crushed car. Then he says, "They all recognized your handiwork, Miss Casselman."

"Thank you," I tell him. It's nice to know I'm appreciated.

But he zeroes in on national news for class discussion: the upcoming program on the Robert Deitz case.

"Somebody tell me about Robert Deitz," Rosenblum says.

"Is that the guy who ate his victims and kept body parts in the refrigerator?" Sharon Rescher-Smith asks.

There's some tittering across the aisles, whether at Sharon or the thought of body parts in the refrigerator I can't be sure.

Rosenblum sighs but answers without looking too impatient. "No, you're thinking of Jeffrey Dahmer."

"Deitz is the guy who killed all those whores," Little-Miss-Know-It-All Melissa Prawel says.

"Prostitutes," Rosenblum corrects her.

Doing a pretty good job of sounding innocently inquisitive, Joanne Tramonto asks, "What's the difference between a whore and a prostitute?"

"Oh, about twenty-five dollars a trick," Gina Mack says.

The answer is so fast and unexpected, I can't help but join in the snickering. Rosenblum loses some of his patient look. "Those women are dead," he tells us.

It's hard to keep a smile on your face after a line like that.

"How did he get caught?" Rosenblum asks.

Nobody wants to say anything, because we're afraid of getting our heads bitten off.

"Miss Liccardi?"

Robin glances around the room as though there could be another Miss Liccardi present. She's the only one in this class from my old grammar school. She shakes her head.

Rosenblum is prowling the room—he never sits at his desk or stays put behind the podium. "Anybody?"

"He returned to the scene of the crime," someone from the back of the room volunteers.

"He returned to the scene of the crime," Rosenblum repeats. "That old chestnut of a plot device in countless murder mysteries, from the fourteenth-century-B.C. Chinese stories of Judge Dee, to Agatha Christie's whodunits written in the 1920s, to last night's cable rerun of *Murder She Wrote*. Which goes to show how cliches and stereotypes sometimes get started: There *is* a kernel of truth."

The class is growing restless as Rosenblum drifts into what should be the English teachers' domain.

"Excuse me," I protest in barely a whisper, "but this is *local,* not *national*."

Rosenblum has wandered close enough to hear, and he's impressed. I rarely volunteer anything in class—even when I'm called on. "Can anybody answer Miss Casselman's question?" he asks.

Not that it was a question—I was just complaining.

"Why is Robert Deitz national news and not local news?" Rosenblum asks the class.

Since Mary Amber DeFranco has global studies third period and isn't here to defend herself, her best friend, Melissa, says, "Because it's on TV."

"Why?" Rosenblum asks. "Why does the crew of a network TV news show come to Port Champlain, New York, to film a documentary about a man who was born here, who lived in this community his entire life until he was sent away to prison, and whose victims lived, worked, died, and had their bodies dumped all within a fifty-mile radius of this very spot?"

That wipes a few grins off faces.

"Prurient curiosity," I mutter.

I see Rosenblum blink in surprise, but at the same time I've spoken, Gina Mack has said, "Because there were so many of them."

Rosenblum chooses to answer her. "Yes," he says.

But then he looks at me. "And yes. In an increasingly violent world, people have become jaded, but even so, *twelve* women dead—one right after the other—for no reason beyond being at the wrong place at the wrong time still attracts attention. Eventually. Do you remember the headlines from two years ago?"

We all look at him blankly.

"Anyone? Miss Carsonne?"

Wakisha looks ready to bluff it but then goes for a reasonable excuse instead. "That was when I was in seventh grade," she tells him. "My seventh-grade teacher didn't have a current events board."

"There *were* no headlines," Rosenblum says, and I can see the relief wash over Wakisha. "Not when the first prostitute was killed. Nor the second. Nor the third. It was about the seventh or eighth before anyone paid attention, when some enterprising soul at the newspaper put together a list—a map—with numbers where bodies had been found to match the pictures of the dead or missing women. As the weeks went by and more bodies were found, the map, the pictures were dragged out again and again. How many women did the *Port Champlain Times* eventually link to this?"

"Twelve," Beatrice—Bertie—Dunbar says, thinking Rosenblum has already supplied the answer.

"Nineteen," Rosenblum corrects. "Deitz confessed to twelve. He was convicted for twelve, but the police have linked nineteen dead or still-missing women to him. The newspapers and news programs were showing the pictures of *nineteen* women dead or missing in a two-year period. Were any of your parents worried about you?"

I say, softly, "My mother was worried about me," but Rosenblum is pacing up and down by the window at this point.

"Was the average Port Champlain woman *really, truly* afraid for her life?" Rosenblum answers his own question because it's obvious he's onto something he thinks is important. "No. Because what was the link?"

"They were all prostitutes," Joanne says.

"I don't think," Rosenblum says, heading back to the front of the room, "that it was a case of: 'They were prostitutes, so they deserved to die.' I *hope* it wasn't a case of that. I *think* it was a case of: 'Thank God it's prostitutes and not children'"—he indicates us, then points to himself—"'or teachers'"—next he makes an expansive gesture to cover everybody—"'or accountants or middle-aged housewives with curly hair' or whatever group whoever was reading the paper belonged to." He brings his fist down, hard, on the podium with uncharacteristic drama. "But bear this in mind: Killers often start on easy prey. With a little bit of practice, they get bolder and bolder, until no one is safe. Remember Hitler: 'Today Austria, tomorrow the world.' Ms. Carsonne,"—we all jump as Mr. Rosenblum flings open the global studies book—"three reasons for feudal Japan's isolation?"

While Wakisha struggles to come up with one, I think of what he's just said: *"No one is safe."*

I think to myself, *Thank God my mother wasn't here to hear that.*

6

After global studies is study hall, and I work very hard to get all my homework done so my mother won't have any legitimate excuse to say I can't go to Cardinal O'Gorman to see about working on the play.

Illegitimate excuses I have no control over.

Tenth period is just a half-hour long, an enrichment course. I've chosen film appreciation, which was described as watching and then discussing classic movies. I figured they meant things like *Star Wars,* and the Kevin Costner version of *Robin Hood,* and *The Outsiders.* Maybe the original *Nightmare on Elm Street.*

But so far there hasn't been a single thing that's even in color, and what we're currently watching is something called *The Grapes of Wrath,* which is this dusty, depressing movie starring Bridget Fonda's grandfather from so long ago that he was too young to *be* anybody's father. The only advantage to these films is that there's four, five, sometimes six classes of watching, and then only one or two of discussing. I nap a lot, and I say things like, "There was a lot of symbolism regarding the Nature of Man."

Connie's older sister says that she took film appreciation when she went to Mother of Sorrows and that they saw *Great Expectations*. I was going to suggest that they show it again this year so I wouldn't have to read it in English, but Connie's sister claims the movie is even worse than the book.

On the bus ride home, I finish my homework, and I feel so virtuous that before dinner I even read a chapter of *Great Expectations*. I only have about seventeen more chapters to go before I catch up to where I'm supposed to be.

7

My cooking expertise ranges from instant rice to macaroni to—on a good day—scrambled eggs.

Wally isn't quite so proficient as I am, so Mom usually does the cooking and Wally and I clean up.

Part of the problem is that Mom's too fussy to give over control. I mean, how much expertise does it take to rinse off some lettuce and chop up a tomato and a stalk of celery? But six years ago, when they were first married, Mom took one look at Wally spritzing the lettuce in the colander and threw him out of the kitchen. Mom practically *scrubs* each piece of lettuce before it goes into the salad bowl.

I wonder what Bryan's psychologist would have to say about that.

Bryan—because he's a poor demented soul—doesn't have any chores, though when Alison and I were his age, we at least were expected to bring our own dishes into the kitchen. But after dinner is Mom and Bryan's "quality time." If I were Grandma Casselman, I'd resent the implication that all that free babysitting she does is somehow substandard time. Like Grandma Casselman has him mowing the lawn or snow blowing the driveway or taking in laundry from the neighbors. Being in kindergarten, Bryan only has a half day, and I know for a fact that sometimes they go to the movies, or the park, or the mall. My bus doesn't drop me off at Grandma's until three, with Mom or Wally picking us up between five and five-thirty. I'm the only fourteen-year-old I know who still gets babysat. Which is a different complaint entirely.

Mom and Bryan spend their after-dinner time reading books together, or Mom will fuss about whatever project he's brought home from kindergarten, or they'll put together a jigsaw puzzle.

Wally's quality time with Bryan is after Mom's, or a bit later, right before Bryan goes to bed. As far as I can tell, my own quality time is when they let me sleep in till eight-thirty or nine on Saturdays.

Meanwhile Wally and I are out in the kitchen, and if Mom ever watched Wally washing dishes, she wouldn't be so concerned about the lettuce.

I decide that my best bet for getting permission to work on the Cardinal O'Gorman play is to get Wally on my side, then have him convince Mom. Wally and I get along pretty well—for an adult and a teenager, that is—despite a rocky start when Alison and I actively conspired to get Mom to dump him and remarry Dad.

So now I realize what I need to do is ease up to the subject real subtly. As I have my back to him, putting dishes away in the cupboard, I ask, "Say, Wally, have you seen any good plays lately?"

Wally pauses to consider. Just as I've decided maybe this wasn't a good opening after all, he says, "Well, about a month ago Bryan and I were at the mall, and there was a little show with people dressed up as Ronald McDonald and the Hamburglar and that purple guy, whoever he's supposed to be."

I get a handful of silverware, which makes a lot of noise as I dry the pieces, one by one—which I usually don't do—and drop them into the drawer. "No, I mean, like a regular play. In a theater." I glance over my shoulder at Wally, but he's concentrating on scrubbing a pot, not looking at me.

"You mean a professional play? Like in New York?"

"Sure," I say. "Or, you know, like a traveling show. Or even an amateur troupe." I use my towel to wipe leftover something-or-other from one of the forks. "Like even a church group might put on, or, say, a school."

At least Alison was never into dramatics, so I don't have to worry about suffering comparisons there.

Wally goes to use the spray hose to rinse off a bulky-handled pot, but the hose catches on something beneath the sink and doesn't come up all the way before starting to spray. Wally squirts himself in the face and chest, then drops the pot onto the floor, upending all the sudsy water that was in the bottom.

I pick up the pot, figuring the safest thing is for me to wipe off as much as I can of the soap residue, and Wally uses the sponge I know Mom uses on the counters to sop up the water from the floor.

"School plays are a lot of fun," Wally says, getting back to the subject I had feared was lost forever. "I was in the drama club in my high school the year we did *The King and I.*"

This is something I never knew about Wally. "Really?" I ask. Wally builds houses. It's hard for me to think of him performing in costume and greasepaint rather than building in bib overalls and sawdust. "Were you the king?" I ask.

Wally laughs, still concentrating on the dishes in the sink. "No, I was one of the palace servants, who kept dropping things and bumping into people and banging my head on the floor when I bowed." He glances at me for the first time, but quickly looks away again. "Intentionally," he assures me. "I was the comic relief."

"Sounds like fun," I tell him. If somewhat painful.

"Mother of Sorrows putting on a play?" Wally asks.

"No."

He places the last of the pots on the drainer and wipes his hands on the corner of my dish towel, then leans against the sink. "Cardinal O'Gorman?" he asks. He's got a twinkle in his eyes: reliving the glory days.

"Yeah," I admit.

"What's the play?"

I realize I never asked Connie. "I'm not sure. I'm not trying out for one of the parts or anything. Connie and I thought we'd volunteer for the backstage crew." Wally starts to nod, starts to say something that would probably have turned out to be, "That sounds like fun, too," but I've got my momentum going and I say, "Sign-up is tonight, but the rehearsals are all after school. Mrs. Miraglia would drive us. And all my homework's done."

Wally hesitates a moment, to make sure I'm really done this time. Then he nods. Choosing his words carefully, he says, "Of course, your mother and I need to discuss this, but, for the moment, I can't see any reason why not."

Everyone *has* to choose words carefully when it comes to my mother.

I throw my arms around him. "Thank you, thank you! I have to know by a quarter to seven; that's when Mrs. Miraglia's coming, *if* she's coming."

Wally gives his slow nod again. "Then I'll talk with your mother now," he says.

"Remind her how good I've been doing in school," I tell him. Interim reports won't be out for another week and a half, so there's little chance of their being able to verify or challenge this. "Tell her I'll keep up with my homework. And my chores. And that it's a good opportunity for me. Tell her how much benefit *you* got from being in a play when you were my age." I'm assuming he *did* benefit.

"All right, all right," Wally laughs. He heads for the living room.

The last thing I see, before I close my eyes and cross my fingers and wish real hard that my mother will be reasonable, is the wet streak that leaning against the sink has left across Wally's rear end.

8

The kitchen door swings shut, and I hear Wally ask Bryan, "Have you and Mommy finished your book? Would you like to shoot a few baskets with me in the driveway?"

Bryan must answer "Yes," even though I don't hear him, because Wally says, "You go ahead and warm up without me. I'll join you in a couple minutes."

I don't know anything about basketball, but I *do* know that our hoop isn't at regulation height, no matter what Wally tells Bryan. The neighbors all have *their* hoops *above* the garage door, not next to it. And even I can tell our basketball is junior-size. But Bryan thinks he's really hot stuff. And he never seems to catch on that he always wins when he plays with Wally, even though the Wentzel kids next door, who aren't that much older than he is, always cream him.

Wally starts out quietly, so I can't hear him, even with my ear pressed against the door. But he obviously hasn't worked up to the subject with the same finesse I did, because in no time at all, I hear Mom's voice cut in.

What Mom says is, "No."

Then she tries to soften this slap-in-the-face negative with a meaningless, "I don't think that would be a good idea."

Wally must ask her, "Why?"

"It's such a commitment of time," Mom says. "Ninth grade is such a big adjustment. It's not like grammar school. She has a lot more homework to do, and studying every night."

My homework's done, I mentally protest. And, as though he's picked up my mental vibrations, Wally says, "Her homework's done."

"Tonight," Mom says. "Susan's not Alison, you know."

Alison skipped third grade—that's what Mom means. She was whatever the grammar school equivalent of valedictorian is when she graduated from Susan B. Anthony School, and she was in all honors and accelerated courses at Lincoln High. What Mom means is "Susan's not as smart as Alison."

Duuuh, I want to say, *but I can walk and chew gum at the same time if I really concentrate.*

I wish I could see the expression on Wally's face as he answers, "Exactly," because Mom backs down real quick. "I can't believe I said that," she says.

"Give her a chance," Wally says. "See how it goes. If she can't keep her grades up, we can always make her drop out." Then he adds, humor in his voice, "Of the play, not school."

Mom doesn't think it's funny. Mom says, "I don't like it,

35

Wally. What kind of supervision do you think there'll be? All those kids roaming the school halls . . ."

Always-calm Wally sounds exasperated. "My God," he exclaims. "What do you think can happen?"

"You know very well," Mom says, "what I think can happen."

"No," Wally insists. "No, I don't."

Then, nothing.

I have to crack the door open just to make sure they're still there. They're sitting on the couch. I had thought maybe Mom was crying, but she's not. She's just sitting there, leaning forward, with her elbows on her knees, leaning her chin on her hands.

"You can't keep her in a stranglehold," Wally says, so quietly I wouldn't have heard with the door closed. "You'll either suffocate her or force her to fight to get free."

Mom shifts position slightly, so that she's resting her forehead in one of her hands, but I still don't think she's crying. Mom doesn't cry easily. She used to, but not anymore.

The phone rings, and I let the door close.

I hear Wally say, "Hello," then he tells Mom, "Ginny Miraglia."

In the time it takes her to get to the phone, I sit down with my back against one of the cabinets and bite my thumbnail so low it bleeds.

Mom's questions sound good; they sound promising: How long are the rehearsals likely to last? Does Connie know any of the people at Cardinal O'Gorman? Will Mrs. Miraglia wait for us or just drop us off? When is the actual play?

Mrs. Miraglia must be giving soothing answers. There's a long period of time when Mom is only saying, "Yes," "All right," and "Uh-huh." Finally, she says, "Thank you."

Thank you sounds encouraging.

Without my hearing her hang up or cross the room, the kitchen door swings open, bumping my leg, and Mom gives me this disapproving look as I scramble to my feet. This nice-girls-don't-eavesdrop look. I've been trying to be a nice girl ever since Alison left, so they won't miss her so much. Some days it comes easier than others.

Mom flutters and hovers, poking at my hair and rearranging my tee shirt, which isn't even what I'm planning on wearing there, and she tells me to behave, and to bring some change in case something happens and I need to call home, and wear a sweater, and I better be darn sure my schoolwork doesn't suffer, and have a good time.

"Thank you, thank you," I tell her, and head for the stairs. What *will* I wear?

"And behave," she repeats.

She repeats it yet again twenty minutes later when Mrs. Miraglia beeps her horn in our driveway and I go flying out the front door: "Behave." Three times. Like a charm.

9

I called Connie specifically to ask her what she was going to wear, and she told me, "Bum-around clothes. We don't know if we're going to be constructing scenery, or painting backdrops, or climbing up to get at the lights, or what."

So I'm wearing the outfit I wore when I decided to redecorate my room in fluorescent green last year: green-spattered sweatshirt (a hand-me-down Halloween shirt proclaiming JUST GIVE ME THE DAMN CANDY that Alison gave me when Mom wouldn't let her wear it trick-or-treating), green-spattered socks (lifted last year from Wally's drawer and he didn't want them back), and green-spattered moccasins with absolutely no tread on them, so I fervently hope we will *not* be required to do any climbing; but you can smell my old sneakers from at least a room away, and I'm not risking my good sneakers or my school shoes.

As soon as I open the car door, however, I see that Connie

is wearing a brand-new jogging suit, stylish gray, with the five interlocking rings of the Olympics. She has her hair up in a gold sparkly scrunchie.

"You said bum-around clothes," I protest, ready to head back to my room to find something more appropriate to wear.

Connie tugs to show that everything fits loosely so she can move around. "Bum-around," she agrees.

"You look fine, dear," Mrs. Miraglia says, which only a mother could say in such a circumstance. Only a mother who doesn't want to wait while I go change.

"Get in," Connie says. "If we're late, all the good jobs will be taken, and we'll be left with clean-up."

I get in, which is obviously a relief for Mrs. Miraglia. She starts the car moving practically before I've got the door closed, so I can't change my mind. "You two are going to have such a good time," she assures us. Then, once we're safely out of the driveway and onto the street, she asks, "What's this play called again?"

Love in the Spotlight, " Connie tells her. "It was a Broadway musical or something."

"Never heard of it," Mrs. Miraglia says.

Neither have I.

"I think it starred somebody like Charlton Heston and Madonna," Connie tells us.

I see Mrs. Miraglia give a startled, skeptical look in the rearview mirror. "Must have been a lean season on Broadway," she mutters.

Mrs. Miraglia drops us off at Cardinal O'Gorman High's front door, which turns out to be locked, and Connie and I cut across the grass to the side door. The ground is mushy from all the rain, and I practically lose my moccasins, besides leaving three-inch-deep footprints. If the Cardinal O'Gorman grounds staff decides that I've ruined their lawn, the police will have dozens of my perfectly preserved footprints with which to identify the culprit.

The side door is open, and the halls are well lit. Someone has put up notebook-paper signs saying TRYOUTS. Arrows direct us to the main hall, and the auditorium doors are open.

Connie and I are a little early. Nobody seems to have taken charge yet.

There is a bunch of kids—boys and girls—gathered around the piano, which is off to the side in front of the stage. The boys keep pushing one another off the piano bench, each trying to get a chance to play, while the girls seem more interested in looking sophisticated as they lounge against the piano. The boys are competing to play things like "Chopsticks" and "Heart and Soul."

More kids are on the stage itself, twirling around or doing cartwheels—playing at being the star. I hate kids who know how to do cartwheels.

There are also quite a few kids sitting in the auditorium—mostly spread out in ones and twos.

I stop suddenly when I spot Alison in the crowd—I recognize her long blond hair from the back—and Connie walks smack into me. I think, *Why is SHE here?* and I feel a bubble of resentment, because if she's here, she'll be better at it than I am, because she's better at everything. And I actually have to remind myself that I should be happy to see her, but by then the girl has turned around enough that I can see it's not Alison after all, no matter *how* I feel.

I sit down fast, in any aisle seat, before Connie can wonder why I stopped so suddenly.

"Uh-oh!" Connie says. "Look who just walked in."

For one awful moment I'm convinced by her tone that it has to be my mother, here to check up on me, but when I look up, I see Mary Amber DeFranco.

She's dressed even better than Connie.

I see her hesitate in the doorway, looking around the auditorium. She must not see anybody else she recognizes, because she heads toward us. "Hi, you guys!" she says in her chirpy little voice, like we're best of friends. "I didn't know you were interested in theater." Instead of sitting on one of the seats, she perches herself on the back of the seat in the row ahead of us. I figure that way she can see all around and notice right away if somebody more interesting comes in.

Mary Amber starts telling us about all the plays she's been in—and it's not grammar school pageants she's talking about: she's been in regional theater. "What parts are you trying out for?" she finally asks. "I mean, obviously we all want to be Leonora, but there are other good parts, too."

I don't tell her I just found out the *name* of the play ten minutes ago. I tell her, "Stagehands."

"Stagehands?" she repeats pensively. "Are you thinking of *Our Town,* with the Stage Manager being the narrator?"

Connie sinks lower into her seat and pretends that she's yawning, not grinning.

"We're not trying out for parts," I tell Mary Amber. "We just want to help backstage."

"Oh," Mary Amber says in a what-kind-of-fool-would-settle-for-that? tone. "You mean like make-up girls and wardrobe assistants?" For all the plays she's been in, it figures she's been totally oblivious to everybody in the crew except those most directly concerned with making her look good.

I'm about to tell her about light and sound systems, and carpenters and painters—all the *little* people—but Connie cuts in. "Yes," she purrs. "Just like that."

"Well, that's nice," Mary Amber gushes. "That's important, too." Like she's saying that we, too, can be useful, productive members of society. She finally spots somebody she knows and abandons us so fast she barely has time to call back, "Toodles."

I do my impersonation of the Queen Mother waving from her carriage to the adoring masses.

The guy Mary Amber has zeroed in on is—to put it as conservatively as possible—gorgeous.

I sigh, louder than I intended.

Connie leans over and whispers to me, "Now *there's* someone you could invite to the dance."

"Yeah," I say, "if Mary Amber is willing to share."

But the gorgeous guy gives Mary Amber an obvious brush-off, and Connie pokes me with her elbow.

"He was looking at *you* before," Connie insists.

Gorgeous goes up to the piano, and hustles the kids away from there, then takes the nearby microphone off the stand. "Hi," he says in this incredibly sexy voice. "For you who don't know me, I'm Matt Burke, a senior here at Cardinal O'Gorman High School, president of the Dramatics Club this year, and assistant director for this production of *Love in the Spotlight*. Welcome, everyone." He says it warmly and sincerely, like he's really delighted we're all here.

"It would be a big help," Matt continues, "if everybody could just move in closer to the stage."

I figure Connie and I are fine right where we are, about fifteen rows back. But Matt looks directly at us and, with a smile, motions us to come closer. "First five rows only," he proclaims.

Connie digs her elbow into my side. "See?" she whispers. "He's interested. Take off your glasses."

"Leave me alone," I say. But I take off the glasses.

10

In comes a sort of young-looking guy wearing jeans and a short-sleeved black shirt with a priest's collar. He leaps onto the stage while we're all shifting forward, and he smiles wide enough to show his molars. *He* doesn't need a microphone. "I'm Father Kevin Romero," he says. "You can call me Father Romero, or you can call me Father Kevin, or you can even call me Father Kev, but please don't call me late for dinner." It's a variation on a joke so old that even Wally has stopped using it.

Connie and I settle down behind a seventeen-year-old midget who's slouched in his seat with a glove balanced on his head, fingers pointing upward. He turns, very, very slowly so as not to tip the glove, and he makes no effort to hide the fact that he's looking us over. "Lincoln?" he asks.

"Mother of Sorrows," Connie answers.

"Ha!" the kid says. "Mossy girls!" Like he's the first person in the world to notice that the initials of Mother of Sorrows

School spell out MOSS. "A rolling stone gathers no moss!" the kid practically shrieks.

"We graduated from grammar school for this?" Connie whispers to me in a very loud whisper.

Before I can answer, Father Kevin says, *"Now,"*—the noise level goes down a few decibels, and the acrobatically inclined kid turns back around, glove still in place. Father Kevin continues—"I think the *best* thing is to get into this *right away*. So, before we get down to assigning *specific* roles, let's *work* on one of the chorus numbers that the *whole group* will be doing. *Here's* the sheet music. OK, everybody *up*."

Connie and I share a distressed look. Obviously we've wandered into the wrong section. Desperation makes me bold. "Ahm, excuse me," I say, but the piano is already playing.

The girl next to me passes me a stack of sheet music, which I pass on to Connie without taking one. Connie hesitates, then takes one before passing the rest on.

"Come *on,* everyone!" Father Kevin shouts. "On your *feet,* settle *in. Listen:* your turn is coming *next*." He's got one of these super-enthusiastic voices that makes me want to bite him.

Connie kicks me because I'm the only one still sitting.

I get up, but I stand with my hands in my pockets, hating Connie already.

The official piano player is a smirky blond kid with no eyelashes. He sings a verse, and Father Kevin says, "Now *every*body. *Share* if there's not enough sheet music."

Next to me, Connie picks up the song quickly, and she has a decent voice.

I move my lips so Father Kevin won't yell at me, but what does a stagehand need to know the songs for?

The whole group plows through the song once, everybody singing melody. Then Father Kevin begins to divide us up: baritones, tenors, altos, sopranos.

I wave my hand in the air, but he ignores me until Connie finally tugs my arm down. "You're going to look like a second grader to Matt," she warns me. "Just wait until Father Kevin gets to us."

It seems like a dumb plan to me. I'm just hoping that—wherever the stage crew is meeting—we won't arrive too late.

Finally Father Kevin gets to our row. "Alto or soprano?" he asks me. Matt Burke is standing next to him with a clipboard, writing down our names and what part we're singing.

"Stage crew," I tell them.

"Yes, yes, I know," Father Kevin says. I guess I just *look* like stage crew. He continues, "But I want *every*body in the spirit of this. Just to give you a *feel* for what we're doing."

"Yes, but—"

He puts his arm around my shoulder. "We're all one *family* here—cast *and* crew. I want everybody to be *happy*."

I'd be happy if he wasn't making a spectacle of me.

"*Alto* or *soprano?*" he asks again.

"I . . ." How should I know? I don't sing. What difference does it make if I don't sing in alto or if I don't sing in soprano?

In music class, Mrs. MacNeely recognizes this. She knows I have just two notes—one high note and one low note. On a really good day, I can squeeze a middle note between the other two. Mrs. MacNeely is happy if I keep the words coming out at the same rate as the other girls.

"Scales, please," Father Kevin says to the pianist, who smirks even more broadly than usual. The rotten kid with the glove—which he's finally removed from his head—is facing backwards, gaping at me. I'm not even looking to see Matt's reaction to all this. I've seen him cross his eyes at some of the other kids' attempts.

"Ah-ah-ah-ah-ah," the pianist sings. "Ah-ah-ah-ah-ah."

I throw a dirty look at Connie, who's beaming. She's always liked being the center of attention. But I figure the only way to get everybody to stop looking at me, including Matt Burke, is to sing the stupid scales.

I hit two of my three notes and Father Kevin says, "Fine! Alto!" and he turns his attention to Connie.

"No need to be nervous," Matt tells me. "You have a really sweet voice."

I get so flustered that I almost give my name as Susan instead of Sibyl.

Connie, of course, is a soprano. All the girls who can sing are sopranos.

This is stupid, I tell myself as we sing in our four-part harmony and I wonder how many of the others are singing only tonight. *What good does it do for us to learn this idiotic song when all we're going to be doing is painting scenery and moving sets around?*

But, on the other hand, Matt *did* call my voice sweet. *Good* would have been a blatant lie, and I would have felt worse because he was obviously trying to make me feel better.

But *sweet?* I suppose it's a possibility.

It keeps me going until nine-thirty, when we break up for the night and Mrs. Miraglia drives me and Connie home.

11

When I get home, Mom greets me like I've just returned home from a three-week camping trip to some war-torn South American country.

Even Wally is showing a tendency to hover.

I assure them that everybody was nice, that I had a great time, that Mrs. Miraglia was exactly where she was supposed to be at exactly the time she was supposed to be there, and that she's a real careful driver, too. I'm just telling them that I haven't been assigned my regular job yet, when the phone rings.

"That'll be for you," Mom says. Which is a surprise, because my friends aren't allowed to call after nine, and it's almost ten.

It turns out to be Dad, calling from California, where it's only seven. "Hi, sweetie," he says. "I hear you're working on your school play."

It didn't take Mom long to tell HIM, I think.

I go through it all again, the way I did for Mom and Wally, imitating Father Kevin's way of stressing every third or fourth word, telling how Connie abandoned me and jumped on the singing bandwagon, and about the ugly blond kid who plays the piano, and the troll with his glove on his head.

But I don't tell any of them about Matt Burke.

12

Despite the fact that my family should have me used to being wound up, I'm so wound up about the play that I have a hard time falling asleep.

The next morning, I have a hard time getting awake.

In fact, I have no clear memory till lunch time, when a bunch of kids are talking about the Robert Deitz documentary that was on TV last night and the gross police photos that were shown of the dead women—some of whom weren't found till six or seven months after they were killed—because the bodies were dumped in rural areas. Fine lunch-time conversation.

Connie is at a different table, working with the other editors on next week's issue of the *Gabriel,* so she isn't around to steer the talk in livelier directions.

Today I have phys. ed., and the sport of the day is volleyball. Coach Merenda breaks us up into four teams that *she* assigns, by the order in which we happened to wander into the gym—which is a heck of a lot easier on me than having team captains that look right through me when there's nobody else left, obviously fervently hoping that there's another girl yet to come out of the locker room.

There are two nets set up at either end of the gym, so we can all play at once. Isn't that a relief?

Bertie Dunbar puts herself in charge of our team. "Stand right here," she tells me. "Lift your arms up, but don't move from wherever you rotate to. If the ball comes near you, one of us will get it."

I salute her and follow her instructions.

As I'm leaving, Coach Merenda tells me, "Simple attendance will get you a D, Sibyl. Some effort is required."

I salute her, too.

I'm looking forward to global studies, because for the current events board I brought in a great article about a window washer whose harness broke. He fell seventeen stories to his death, while his wife—who worked in the office building across from where he was cleaning—watched.

But instead of selecting my article to discuss, Mr. Rosenblum chooses Carolyn Tumia's sports article. Everybody knows that Rosenblum's favorite football team is the Cleveland Browns—he talks about them enough—and they played a game last night and won. Mr. Rosenblum gives us a lecture on the history of football, with all those silly position names. I mean, there's a player who's called a *nose tackle:* that doesn't even bear thinking about.

We get back at Rosenblum by pretending we can't remember the name of the Browns, referring to them as the Cleveland Tans or the Ohio Beiges.

In study hall, Ms. LaMond corners me when I hand her the sign-up sheet. "Susan," she says brightly, and I can tell what's coming. "How's Alison doing?"

Ms. LaMond was Alison's eighth-grade teacher at Susan B. Anthony School—except that she was *Miss* LaMond then. Miss LaMond kept telling Mom and Wally how much creative talent Alison had, and she even submitted her name to Lakeside School of the Arts for a scholarship. Alison won the scholarship, of course, but it was only for about a third of the tuition, and our family didn't have enough for the rest. Miss LaMond was devastated that Alison ended up going to Abe Lincoln High.

I was lucky enough never to get Miss LaMond: If *Mom* thinks I'm a dummy compared to Alison, what would Alison's *teacher* think? She left the year after she had Alison in class; she got married to a guy whose company was transferring him to Colorado.

But now it's five years later and she's suddenly back, and she's Ms. LaMond, not Miss LaMond and not Mrs. Van Strydonk, and here she is at Mother of Sorrows, overseeing my study hall and asking me about Alison.

"Nothing new," I tell her. "She called last week, and I told her you'd been asking about her."

Ms. LaMond recognized my name the first day, way back in September, and asked me then where Alison was going to college.

So I told her that Alison hadn't been able to decide, and that she and a girlfriend had an apartment in New York, where they took special classes from artists and auditioned for parts in plays.

"How exciting," Ms. LaMond had said, sighing. "Oh, to be that young and that carefree!"

But lately she wants to know if Alison is any closer to choosing a *regular* art college—like, for example, Pratt Institute, for which Ms. LaMond would be happy to write a recommendation—because talent is one thing, but an education is forever.

I consider lying to her: telling her that Alison *has* settled on a college—one in Kansas, or Montana, or Brazil. But, with my luck, whatever I chose would turn out to be Ms. LaMond's alma mater, or she'd be best buddies with the department head there, or somehow or other she'd catch me at it. So I just shrug.

Ms. LaMond goes to her desk and gets out a big manila envelope full of college brochures. She's even attached postage. "Send these to her," she tells me. "Or give them to her, the next time she comes home for a vacation."

I assure her I will.

"Little Alison Casselman, all grown up and living on her own in New York," she says with a sigh, that sigh adults give when kids make them feel particularly old.

"With a girlfriend," I correct her.

But Ms. LaMond hasn't even heard me. "I'll bet she turned out to be a beautiful young woman," she says.

I figure she means Alison, not the girlfriend.

I tell her I have a picture in my wallet, and she has me get it out of my purse. Alison has this incredible blond hair that cascades in perfect ripples past her shoulders; her eyes are wide and blue and innocent, but her smile is just a little mischievous.

"Oh, she is," Ms. LaMond says. "She *is* beautiful."

I figure nobody will ever say that about me. The best I can hope for is "You have a sweet voice."

"Is this her senior picture?" Ms. LaMond asks.

I say yes, even though it was taken in Alison's junior year, because it's faster and easier to agree than to explain.

Ms. LaMond hands me back my wallet, and I go back to my seat.

In film appreciation, I finally get to put my head down on my desk and go to sleep.

13

After school, Connie and I walk to Cardinal O'Gorman. I consider myself lucky that Mom hasn't told me that I have to call her at work to verify that I've successfully completed the ten-minute journey from Mother of Sorrows to Cardinal O'Gorman.

There's absolutely nobody in the backstage area, so Connie and I sit, once again, in the auditorium with everybody else. I look around to find Matt Burke to ask him about where we're supposed to go to sign up for the stage crew, but there's no sign of him.

The rehearsals are every afternoon, but I figure maybe the stage crew won't meet that often. *That* would please my mother, but I find myself disappointed at the thought. There's a certain energy and excitement to this crowd, I have to admit, which is sort of fun—which is dumb because they have that energy and excitement because they're singers and actors, and

I'm not. I'll also miss not being here every day because that means from now on I'll probably only catch an occasional glimpse of Matt, and that's even dumber because I can picture myself with a vacant, moony expression, gazing at him adoringly while he's looking at me with a puzzled, am-I-supposed-to-know-you? frown. How demeaning!

Somebody touches my arm—I'm sitting on an aisle seat—and it's Matt and he's smiling at me and Connie, and he says, "I'm glad you came back."

Thank goodness he moves on before I can get any sounds out, because all I accomplish is some scattered meaningless syllables.

Connie smacks my arm and says, "Take your glasses off."

I take my glasses off, even though he seems to be telling *everyone* he's glad they came.

We stand to follow Matt, but by then he's dashed up the side stairs onto the stage, and somebody else is there. Without my glasses I can't even make out Connie right next to me, much less who's on stage, but I recognize Father Kevin's booming voice.

"I know there are those of you who are *primarily* interested in helping *backstage,* but today we're going to be learning a few basic dance steps, and I think it'd be a *good idea* for all of you to participate, so *everybody* knows *exactly* where we're *coming from.*"

Where we're coming from?

I put my glasses back on, quickly.

We gather on stage around a seventy-year-old woman who introduces herself as Mrs. Fallahi, a friend of Father Kevin's, and our dance instructor. Connie and I exchange relieved glances. How bad could this possibly be?

Then Mrs. Fallahi introduces us to three dancers from her studio who are going to be helping us out: Sigrid, Evangeline, and Crysta. The girls are between five-five and five-seven feet tall; none of them looks to be a hundred pounds. They pull off their wraparound skirts and are all wearing shiny, skin-tight leotards. And they all look good in them. Sigrid has her blond hair in a french twist, Evangeline's auburn hair is in a french braid, and Crysta has about a hundred cornrow braids, each with a tiny golden bell at the end. It takes the boys in the group the rest of the afternoon to pull their eyeballs all the way back into their sockets and to consistently remember to keep their jaws up and breathe through their noses, not their mouths.

Oh yeah, I think, before we do a single dance step. *This could be real bad.*

14

At dinner, Mom and Wally quiz me on (a) Do I have a lot of homework? (by which they mean: Am I likely to get it all done before bedtime?) and (b) How did rehearsal go?

No and fine, I tell them.

They're not satisfied; they want to know more.

I don't tell them that, judging by the conversation at lunch, we seem to be just about the only family in the area who didn't watch and/or record the Robert Deitz documentary. But I'm tempted—it would be a good diversionary tactic—as Mom keeps asking: Did any of your friends besides Connie sign up? How many people are there? Where do they come from be-sides Mother of Sorrows and Cardinal O'Gorman? Are they mostly freshmen or upperclassmen? Do most of them seem to have experience in this sort of thing? Are the adults Cardinal O'Gorman faculty?

I give her the benefit of the doubt: I assume she's making

polite conversation to show she's interested and she doesn't re-alize that she sounds like a police interrogator. Even Wally's eyes are beginning to glaze over.

Finally, Bryan decides he's been ignored long enough. "Hey, what about me?" he demands. "I need to know I'm as important to you as Susan is." Which is obviously something he's taken verbatim off of one of his psychologist's checklists.

But at least it gets Mom and Wally off my back.

15

At lunch, Connie tells everyone what a good time we're having working on the play. She does imitations of Father Kevin and the smirky blond pianist and Mary Amber DeFranco and a bunch of the other people. She even makes fun of Mrs. Fallahi's three dancers. Twisting her hair away from her face, she sucks in her cheeks to give herself that artsy gaunt look, then she sticks her nose in the air and says, in a pseudosophisticated accent, "I am Sigrid. Watch me dance."

The way she tells it, it sounds like fun even to me.

Then she tells everyone that Matt Burke is obviously crazy about me.

"Yeah, right," I say. "He's nice to everybody," I tell them.

"No, really," Connie insists. "He came up to me while you were in the bathroom and asked about you."

"You didn't tell him I was in the bathroom, did you?" I ask, though in all probability Matt must realize even Sigrid uses the bathroom.

Connie shakes her head.

"What did he say?" I and half the table ask, all at the same time.

"He said," Connie says, lowering her voice and getting that excited look on her face, "he said, 'Excuse me, is that your sweater?'"

The rest of the table waits expectantly.

Finally, I ask, "Yeah?"

"Well, obviously he knew it was *yours*."

"Yeah?" I repeat.

"So," Connie says triumphantly.

"Connie," I say, "even if he *did* know it was mine—so what?"

"He was just asking to hear me say it," Connie insists. She says the name slow and dramatic, the way it's supposed to be: "It's *Sybil's* sweater."

"What'd he say next?" Wakisha demands.

I turn on her. "This is *my* story," I remind her. I ask Connie, "What'd he say next?"

"He started to ask if Mrs. Fallahi could borrow it, but meanwhile Crysta called over that she'd found one."

Sharon Rescher-Smith looks skeptical. "I don't know . . ." she starts.

Wakisha smacks her arm. "It's Sibyl's story."

"Doesn't sound like much to me," I have to admit.

"You're missing the point," Connie says. "Crysta found a sweater to borrow about three rows from the stage. Matt came halfway into the auditorium to ask me about *your* sweater.

Surely he passed by a whole bunch of sweaters to get to yours. He just wanted to hear me say your name, and to touch your sweater."

Everybody makes those self-pleased "Ooooo" sounds that we learned in first grade and that are designed to make the recipient cringe.

"Trust me," Connie says. "He's enamored of you." She's in honors English, which is reading *Romeo and Juliet*, otherwise even *she* wouldn't use phrases like "enamored of you."

Well, I tell myself, *it's a possibility. Though he IS nice to everybody,* I remind myself. I try to think back to which sweater I was wearing, then remember it was my Bugs Bunny one that's been through the wash about seven hundred times.

It could be better, I think.

But, on the other hand, Connie's right: it's distinctive enough that Matt *had* to have known it was mine.

It's a thought that keeps me warm all through science lab, where we measure the tensile strength of rubber bands; and through global studies, where Mr. Rosenblum ignores the newspaper article I've brought in about a woman who was electrocuted while loading wet clothes into a dryer her husband had tried to fix by himself; and into study hall, where Ms. LaMond says to me, "You didn't mail off that packet of information to Alison yet, did you?"

I try to figure which is what she wants, yes or no, before deciding which I should answer.

But before I get a chance to work it out, she hands me a flyer. "I just found out about this art contest," she tells me.

"It's open to everyone, and the prize is five hundred dollars. Once Alison enrolls in a college, she could certainly use five hundred dollars for books and supplies."

Just assuming Alison would win. Which she probably would.

"Alison has always been good at drawing people," Ms. La-Mond says, "which, of course, is absolutely the hardest thing. And she does great babies, not too cartoony, not *too* cute."

I presume this has something to do with something, and I glance at the flyer. The contest is to design a poster for the Port Champlain Right-to-Life Fund. "This looks just like Alison's sort of thing," I agree, glad to hear that my voice is working.

"And it might be just the thing to push Alison into making a decision about college," Ms. LaMond adds, obviously well pleased with herself.

"Good idea," I tell her. "I left the package from yesterday with my mom, so I don't know if she mailed it yet. But even if she has, I'll put this in an envelope and get it off to her tonight."

I can see that my sisterly concern has brought me up in Ms. LaMond's estimation. If she could see inside to what I really am . . . But she can't, I reassure myself. She beams at me, and I go back to my seat.

After study hall, Gina Mack asks me, "What's with you and Ms. LaMond? How come the two of you are always chatting before class?"

"She knows my sister," I explain. "She's always asking about her."

"I didn't know you had a sister," Gina says.

There're a lot of things Gina doesn't know. She's never even been to my house, or me to hers. But for some reason I find myself bringing out Alison's picture from my wallet. "This is Alison," I say. "She moved away from home."

"Yow," Gina says, looking at the picture. "That'll make you feel like something the cat dragged in."

I can't even smack her, because she's exactly right.

Which pretty well cools off the rest of the warm feeling I'd been carrying around since lunch.

16

That afternoon, as Connie and I are walking to Cardinal O'Gorman, I tell her, "I've been thinking about me and Alison."

Connie's been my best friend so long that she even remembers my dad, who moved out when Connie and I were in kindergarten. Over the years, she's spent more time at our house than my brother Bryan's accumulated in his five years. So Connie knows Alison, and she asks, "What, specifically?"

I pull out the picture I seem to keep flashing these past few days.

Connie gives a noncommittal grunt.

"How come she looks like that and I look like this?" I complain.

"You look fine," Connie assures me.

"Now you sound like my mother," I tell her. "How do you think I'd look with Alison's hair?"

"You mean you kept it when she left?" Connie says. A second

later she gasps. "I'm sorry," she says. "I meant that as a joke . . ."

"I took it as a joke," I assure her, which I did, until she started hyperventilating.

"Sorry," she insists. "Me and my big mouth."

I shrug.

"Were you thinking about the style?" Connie asks. "Or do you want to lighten your color?"

I consider. I was *thinking* about the whole package. Frequently, when I don't hate Alison, I want to be her. "I don't know. I need to do *some*thing."

"Cut," Connie recommends. "Shaped."

She says it so fast and so enthusiastically I have to point out, "You said I looked fine now."

"You'll look finer," she tells me.

By then we've reached Cardinal O'Gorman, and I let the subject drop. I'm thinking I've *got* to find Matt Burke or Father Kevin to let them know it's really time for Connie and me and the rest of the stage crew to separate from the performers.

But as we're entering the school, the boys' soccer team is coming out. They start showing off for us, and some of them are kind of flirting, and some of them are kind of cute.

By the time Connie and I get into the auditorium, everybody else is on stage, reviewing the song we learned two days ago. Father Kevin interrupts the piano player to call across the auditorium, "Come *on*, girls, you're *late*," so that everybody is looking at us. Now is not the time to start an argument with him, so Connie and I meekly take our places on stage.

Mrs. Fallahi also tells us to hurry up. She adds that we're about to put the singing and the dancing together. Oh joy.

The whole thing is a mess. How in the world can anybody count the dance beats while they're singing words that have nothing to do with left, left, left, kick, then slide, then turn, then left arm out, and reverse?

Of course, I'd had a ballet phase when I was younger—just about every girl has either a ballet phase or a horse phase—but even then I'd been more promising as ballet *audience* material than as a ballet *dancer*. Besides, nobody expects a ballerina to be singing while she's doing her grand jetés across the stage.

I'm determined to bail out, and I think to myself, *Thank God I won't be doing this again.*

After we've spent enough time crashing into each other and into the back and side curtains, Father Kevin says for the chorus to take a break; he wants to talk to the kids who are trying out for the major roles.

Connie says she needs to get a drink or she'll die, but I tell her I'm not letting Father Kevin out of my sight. I really need to talk to him as soon as possible. Connie shrugs and deserts me. Father Kevin is over by the piano, auditioning Mary Amber DeFranco and a bunch of the other talented kids.

I'm sitting on the edge of the stage, dangling my legs over the edge—as far away as I can get from the piano so there'll be no chance of Father Kevin thinking that I want to try out and having to embarrass both of us by telling me I'm not qualified. This is stage left, we've been instructed just today, with the directions being as though facing the audience: stage left, stage right, upstage—which is by the back curtain—and downstage—closest to the audience. I'm feeling very professional in my new knowledge.

This short, skinny kid with an incredible amount of wild rusty hair walks in from backstage, and I think to myself in this vague sort of way, *Who IS this kid?* because he looks sort of familiar. He looks up from the clipboard he's carrying and I realize that I recognize him from the first night. He was sitting next to Stan, the troll with the glove on his head—who's lost the glove but still calls me "mossy girl." But this guy hasn't been here since. *A dropout,* I think. *He hasn't experienced Mrs. Fallahi yet.*

But now he walks right up to me and asks if I would mind walking across the stage so he can test out the spots.

"The what?" I ask.

"The spotlights," he says. "I want to see if they'll track somebody all the way across the stage."

Whatever.

I get up and walk across the stage while the curly-haired kid yells instructions to somebody in the balcony. The light comes on and jiggles in a line that more or less keeps me lit from upper stage left to the center footlights then off right.

The kid with the clipboard is scribbling notes, and I'm getting a funny feeling in my stomach. "Ahm, excuse me," I say, and he looks up, "but are you who I think you are?"

He considers for a moment before saying, quizzically, "Spencer Pabrinkis?"

"No, I mean, are you guys the lighting crew?"

Spencer Pabrinkis looks relieved that this is an easy question. "Oh," he says. "Yes. I—"

I don't wait to hear a word more. I stalk off the stage, looking for Matt Burke, because I don't dare yell at a priest, even if I *am* Lutheran.

I head for the cafeteria, which is where everybody said they were going. As soon as I enter, Connie calls out, "Sibyl!" She's sitting on the window ledge next to Matt. As soon as I see him, I realize I can't yell at him either.

But I *am* still planning on complaining, forcefully.

Except Connie's demanding, "Where've you been?" She gets up and navigates me into the tiny space between her and Matt. This leaves me crunched and at an awkward angle.

"How's it going?" Matt asks, flashing a mind-numbing smile. Or at least it's numbing my mind. "You're all looking super."

"Thank you," I say, wondering if my glasses are clean, wondering if it's too late to take them off now.

Matt downs the last of his pop and tosses the can into the recycling bin. "Sorry," he says, leaping to his feet, "gotta set up for the next number. Catch you later, right?"

"I . . ." I start, but he's already halfway across the room.

Connie jabs me with her elbow. "Why didn't you talk to him?" she demands. "How're you ever going to get him to ask you out if you don't talk to him?"

I'm ready to upend her can of pop over her head, but I control myself. "Do you see all these people we don't know?" I ask instead. "They're the crew. *The crew's already been chosen.*"

"Well," Connie says. "So?"

"It was a test: the ones who had the brains to say no the first night got what they wanted; the rest of us got sucked into the cast. Well, I'm quitting."

"Don't be silly," Connie says. "Do you want to upset Matt?"

I'm trying to think of the most tactful way to tell Connie that she's completely out of her mind, when she says, "Come on. All they need is extra warm bodies. In the chorus you don't need to know how to sing or dance. It'll be fun."

"Yeah," I say, realizing that my best friend has just told me I'm a no-talent who couldn't be in a production that demanded more than breathing.

"And you'll get to see more of Matt if you're in the cast than if you're on the crew."

I sigh. "Whatever happens from now on," I tell her, "remind me that I deserve it."

17

That night I announce to my family that I'm no longer part of the stage crew for *Love in the Spotlight* but part of the cast, and also that I want to do something different with my hair.

Mom and Wally are in favor of both.

Bryan doesn't care about either.

18

Thursday morning in homeroom, I try to talk Wakisha into letting me put up an article I found for world news. I've also brought one from the local section, my regular assignment, since Wakisha had no way of knowing I'd find something so perfect, but now she's giving me a hard time.

Wakisha—being Catholic and also a suck-up—has brought some long article about a trip the pope is taking.

I, on the other hand, have found an article about a teacher at a school in England—a male teacher, named of all things Mr. Rosenblatt—who apparently became a militant vegetarian after his wife came down with and died from Mad Cow Disease. When the headmistress—I love that word, *headmistress*—refused to take him seriously, he tied her up and tried to cram her into the school lunchroom oven, to make a point about something, I guess. Maybe that it's good not to be a cow, mad or otherwise. Luckily the headmistress was what the newspaper diplomatically called an ample woman, so the teacher had trouble getting her in and help arrived before he got more than her headmistressy rump into the oven.

I have added an editorial comment to the space around the article. I have written: "In some cases it pays not to teach men how to cook."

"I can't put that up!" Wakisha protests. "That's the stupidest thing I ever read. What would Mr. Rosenblum say?"

"That's what I'm trying to find out," I tell her. "If you don't want to take credit for it, you can tell him this one is yours." I hand her the local article, about a kid who died after being in a coma since the last day of summer vacation, when he'd been horsing around and fell out of his seat in a ferris wheel.

Wakisha shakes her head and gives a long, drawn-out "Naaaah," with her nose wrinkled, as if the article smells bad. "That's more your kind of thing, Sibyl."

"OK," I tell her.

She looks at me suspiciously, but I just tuck the English-headmistress article into my skirt pocket, and I don't say another thing about it, even when Rosenblum comes to check out the current events board.

I'll have a chance to put it up after lunch.

19

As soon as I walk into global studies, Mr. Rosenblum crooks his finger at me in a come-here gesture and gives a tight smile that's positive proof that he's either guessed that the English-headmistress article is my handiwork or Wakisha's told him for sure. She'd make a terrible spy: she'd spill her guts at the first sight of electrodes.

"Trying for extra credit, Miss Casselman?" he asks, tapping his finger on the current events board.

Actually, I'm surprised to see it still up. Rosenblum has another global studies class seventh period, and I would have thought he'd have taken it down then. But maybe he figured that once the first girl saw it, everybody would be talking about it anyway. He looks more annoyed than angry, so I risk asking him, "*Is* it worth extra credit?"

He flashes another tight smile. "No." He crosses his arms over his chest, ignoring all the girls who are crowding around the current events board—more attention than that corner's gotten since Gail Kraynik pinned up a picture of a Libyan terrorist who bore an uncanny resemblance to Sister Carlotta. Over the ringing of the second bell, he asks, "*Was* there a purpose to bringing this article in?"

"You always say that if there's anything we don't understand, we should ask," I remind him.

"I also say there's no such thing as a dumb question," Rosenblum says, hinting that maybe his life philosophy might be ready for some changes. "*Is* there something you wanted to ask?"

"Yes," I tell him. "I was wondering why you always ignore *my* articles."

I think I've taken him by surprise, because he just looks at me blankly.

"I bring in good local articles," I say, "and you always pick world news and national news. Last time, when I had world news, you always picked national news or local news to discuss." I mean, I can understand that *sports* is a dead end, but he seems to be making a conscious effort to ignore me.

"Miss Casselman," Rosenblum says, "the articles you choose don't tend to lend themselves to discussion. When you did world news, as I recall, you concentrated on tidal waves and plane crashes and people struck by lightning."

I nod, pleased that he has been—after all—paying attention. "I'm working to a theme," I explain.

"Ah," Rosenblum says. "And that theme is . . . ?"

I clear my throat, to make sure I have everyone's attention, because what I have to say is so important. "Life," I tell them, "is a series of random accidents, the last of which is fatal."

Mr. Rosenblum hesitates, as though he expects I might speak again. Finally he nods, once—more to acknowledge, I think, than to necessarily indicate agreement. "Thank you," he says slowly. He stares at the current events board: Wakisha's article about the pope's trip, Mary Amber's article about a senator being investigated for accepting bribes, Carolyn's article about some cheerleaders' exhibition, and mine about the idiot who fell from the ferris wheel. Rosenblum takes a deep breath. "Does anyone know how ferris wheels came to be named?" he asks.

20

During film appreciation, I get a note from the office telling me to go down to the guidance office.

Alison, I think. But I force myself to stop thinking it.

After all, I tell myself, *it was only film appreciation. If the nuns pulled me from religion—THAT would be something to worry about.*

Mrs. Owen, the guidance counselor, sits at her desk, wearing a smile that's professional, but too cheerful and encouraging for really bad news. She has her hands clasped on top of some papers that are on her desk, and I notice that her nails are long and well shaped and polished. I work to convince myself that no one who is about to deliver a truly awful message would worry about having well-manicured nails.

"How are things going, Susan?" she asks, motioning for me to sit down.

"Sibyl," I correct her.

"Excuse me?" she says.

"Please call me Sibyl."

"Sibyl Casselman?" she asks, to make sure she has the right student. The school is big, and there's no way she can know all the students. The guidance office mostly concentrates on juniors, trying to help them decide on colleges and get grants and scholarships. "I'm so sorry." She moves her hands and stares at the top page. "How silly." She reaches for a pen. "They've mistakenly gotten your name as Susan."

"It *is* Susan," I tell her. "But I prefer Sibyl."

She smiles and says, "Of course." She hesitates, then puts the pen back without making any notation. She continues to smile at me. "So, how are things going, Sibyl?"

"OK," I tell her, wondering if my mother has been panicking again.

Mrs. Owen's expression becomes a bit more serious—she's into sincere and concerned mode. "Is anything bothering you?"

Should I say "no" immediately, indicating I don't even have to think about it, or should I pause so I don't sound too eager to deny having problems?

"No," I say immediately but slowly.

She says, "I ask because there's some feeling among the teachers that there might be something bothering you."

Rosenblum, I think. Rosenblum has blown me in, not Mom after all. "No," I assure her.

Again she smiles at me. "Just checking."

"Uh-huh." I like her better for the touch of amusement in her voice when she says "Just checking," so I don't ask her if she's checking individually with each of the students at Mother of Sorrows.

"Anything you'd like to talk about?" she asks me.

"No," I tell her.

"We want you to be happy."

"Well, good," I say. "I want me to be happy, too." I grin to show her how happy I am.

She smiles again but rapidly counters with, "Any problems at home?"

I shake my head.

Together we listen to the clock on her desk tick.

I decide to give her something, just to get out of here before the final bell, before Connie has to come looking for me to walk to Cardinal O'Gorman together, so I say, "Except . . ."

She leans forward in her chair.

"I'm working in the Cardinal O'Gorman play, *Love in the Spotlight*. It's very exciting. But I haven't gotten enough sleep this week. That's all: I'm just a little bit tired. I'm still trying to get the balance between making enough time for rehearsals and making enough time for studying so my grades don't suffer."

Mrs. Owen smiles reassuringly, but I can see she doesn't buy this for a second, probably because she's seen my interim reports. "Well, theater can be a worthwhile outlet," she says. "Very stimulating. A chance to meet new people, try out new ideas, stretch. But you're right: balance is the key. Don't let yourself get over-tired by trying to do too much."

"OK."

"And I'm always here," she says. "If you want to talk."

"OK."

Yeah, right. Like I want to talk to someone who has to look up my name on a sheet.

"Or your teachers," she adds as though she's read my mind.

"OK." I think I might eventually feel a grudging liking for her. So long as she doesn't call my mother.

21

Father Kevin announces who gets the main roles—Mary Amber *is* chosen for the female lead, Leonora; and Mrs. Fallahi announces who will be the front line of dancers. Besides Sigrid, Evangeline, and Crysta, of course.

Then Father Kevin and Mrs. Fallahi put their heads together and come up with a plan of who'll stand where for the chorus numbers. It's a delicate blend, balancing talent against height. Connie ends up in the first row, the last one on the right. I end up in the second row because I have no sense of rhythm but am the shortest one here. There are two more rows behind me.

"Don't worry," Matt Burke assures us. "Everybody will be able to see all of your faces because the set people are making risers for you to stand on."

"Terrific," I mutter to the girl next to me. "Some idiot's sure to fall off during 'Sunshine in May.'" I mean, of course, me.

Naturally, once they change our positions for the dance numbers, the singing suffers, especially for the altos—which is where they dumped anybody who couldn't sing to begin with. As soon as we can no longer hear each other, most of us can't keep to our parts any longer. We just sort of blend in with the sopranos or the tenors or the baritones—whomever we happen to be standing next to at the time. Does Andrew Lloyd Webber have these problems?

"OK," Father Kevin announces as we learn a new song. "You're going to have helium balloons tied to your wrists for this number. But for now, just move your arms up and down like this. That's the way."

While we're all concentrating on moving our arms up and down, Mrs. Fallahi bangs her hand on the top of the piano. "You're losing the beat," she yells at us. "One, two, three, *slide*! *Left* arm on hip, *then* turn."

"Stop mumbling," the music director breaks in—I never *have* learned his name. "You've got to learn these words. Altos, I can't hear you."

"Lights!" Matt shouts. "Spence, what's going on? You're supposed to have blues on the back row."

And, of course, "Smile," they keep reminding us. "Look like you're having a wonderful time."

"How can we sing the words and count out the dance steps and smile all at the same time?" those of us in the back three rows ask. Apparently it's not a question that bothers the front-line people at all. Apparently they don't notice what an incredibly stupid play *Love in the Spotlight* is.

As we're leaving the auditorium for our break, Spencer, the kid with the weird hair, the one in charge of the lights, passes by me and he kind of mumbles, "You always smile nice."

"See what three thousand dollars and the right orthodontist can do for you?" Connie says. She grabs my arm. "Come on, Sibyl, I saved some pop for you and Matt."

I turn to give Spencer a see-you-later, but he's already disappeared backstage.

"And *talk to Matt*," Connie says. "You've got to loosen up."

But as soon as we get to the break room, Matt starts talking to Connie about the speaking part she's just today been assigned, a small but crucial role as Jasmine Dawn, who almost comes between the two leads, Willard and Leonora.

"So," I say the third time Connie kicks me and the first time neither she nor Matt is talking when she does so, "what subjects do you take, Matt?"

Connie rolls her eyes at my originality. She doesn't give Matt a chance to answer. "Somebody was just telling Sibyl what a nice smile she has, Matt. Don't you think she has a nice smile?"

"Super," he agrees.

"Great," I say. "I can't sing. I can't dance, but I can smile. Maybe I should just stand in the wings and grin at the audience for the whole show."

Matt is drinking from his pop can and doesn't answer.

Mary Amber, our very own star, runs in waving pom-poms. "Oh, look what just came in! Aren't these simply great? The prop people just brought in three boxes." She shakes a pom pom in my hair.

Obviously, I think, a closet cheerleader. I hate cheerleaders.

"Super," Matt says. "Gotta run, Connie. Sibyl."

He goes off with Mary Amber to share in the excitement of pom-poms.

Once they're gone, Connie gives me a disgusted look. "Not too good," she says.

I give my three-thousand-dollar smile. "Super."

"He's interested," she insists. "He's ready. All you've got to do is act halfway normal."

"Interested?" I repeat. "He's more interested in *you* than me."

Connie looks shocked. "No," she says. But, being Connie, she can't help but steal a glance in one of the mirrors, and she fluffs her hair. "No," she repeats. "I'm only talking to him for your sake."

"I'm depressed," I tell her.

"*Do* something about it," she tells me.

"What? Prozac? Valium?"

"Whatever happened to that new hairdo you were going to get?"

I think about it. I get out Alison's picture and think about it until Father Kevin yells, "Places, everybody!"

22

At home, Mom asks, "What happened in school today?"

I start to tell her about the pom-poms, and she interrupts me and says, "No, in school."

Mrs. Owen.

I say, "Nothing much."

Mom says, "I got a call from a Mrs. Owen in the guidance office."

Well, duh. I'd already figured that out. "What does she want?" I ask innocently.

"She's worried that you aren't happy."

"They have quotas to fill," I tell her. "They were pulling in all the girls. If they don't talk to a certain number of us every month, their jobs get cut."

"She asked if there were any changes going on at home, and I said no. But then I started wondering if this has anything to do with Alison moving out three years ago."

"They even called Connie into the office," I say, "and asked her if *she* was happy. You know Connie—she'd have a smile on her face if she was brain dead."

Mom tries to figure out if that calls for a smile or a reprimand. "OK," she says slowly.

"Quotas," I repeat.

She nods, but doesn't say anything.

23

In homeroom on Friday, Mr. Rosenblum hands out our class pictures that were taken at the beginning of the school year.

Need I say more?

I remember fighting with the photographer, who kept telling me to smile. "I *am* smiling," I snarled, at the exact moment the flash went off.

So here I am, with my lips curled back from my clenched-together teeth, looking like a *National Geographic* portrait of an aggressive chimpanzee. The hair on the right side of my head is properly poofy, but there's a flat spot just left of my part.

I rest my head on my desk and Anne-Marie Torelli asks me what's the matter. "Rotten picture," I say.

"Let me see." She picks up one of the sheets of pictures—Mom ordered the deluxe package so she would have enough pictures to include in all the Christmas cards—and says, "Oh, you mean because your top button is undone and your collar is bent under? Your bra strap hardly shows at all."

I check the picture and sigh.

When I get home, sweaty and tired and cranky from rehearsal, I ask Mom if I can please have something done with my hair. I'm ready to whine and beg for immediate attention, but she agrees so quickly that I have to wonder how long I've looked so bad that even my mother has noticed.

Saturday afternoon my mother and I go to Snip 'n' Curl at the mall. I've been assigned to a hairdresser named Meriel, whose hair is about five shades lighter than her eyebrows, and her eyebrows seem locked in a perpetually superior arch. Meriel asks what I want done, and I tell her I don't know.

She plunks me down with a stack of books to search through. The majority of the pouty-faced models look as though they're auditioning for Calvin Klein ads. I don't know where women wear hairstyles like that, but it's definitely not Port Champlain.

Meriel putters a bit at her station, swishing combs through disinfectant, getting the kinks out of the cords of her blow-dryer and curling iron. Then she comes back. "Finding any-thing, hon?" she asks me.

My mother has started glancing at her wristwatch, trying to be unobtrusive.

"Do you have any regular magazines?" I ask. I'm hoping for *Seventeen* or *TV Guide.* Even *Modern Maturity* has to have better stuff than what Meriel has shown me so far.

Meriel finds a dog-eared copy of *Cosmopolitan*. As I flip through it, she asks me, "Are you looking for something short, or layered, or contoured? A blunt cut? Something sleek, or to add volume? Sporty? Glamorous? Romantic? Dramatic? Easy-care?" I'm sure my expression is beginning to show my growing panic at all these options. "Bangs?" Meriel asks, which certainly *seems* like a straightforward question.

"I don't know," I admit.

Meriel watches another girl walk into the salon and get assigned to one of the other hairdressers. The girl has brought a picture with her. The other hairdresser nods and leads her to the back area to wash her hair. Meriel is obviously going to have a serious talk with the receptionist who assigned me to her. "Do you just want a trim," she asks, "or a perm?"

"What do *you* recommend?" Mom asks.

"Perm," Meriel says, as in: "No question."

Neither I nor Alison has ever had a perm. If my mother ever has, it was too long ago for me to remember. Now my mother says, "That might be fun for a change."

Meriel looks doubtful. Meriel *knows* she isn't going to have any fun at all until I'm out of here.

"How about," Mom suggests, "if I go do some shopping? I can come back in an hour or so?"

"Two," Meriel says, "if she gets a perm."

"I don't want to look like Grandma Casselman," I say. I love my grandmother, but her hair—besides being a pinkish rust color unlike anything in nature—is a single mass of tight little curls.

Meriel laughs. "Trust me," she says. "There're all kinds of perms."

I nod to my mother, and she kisses my cheek, right there in the middle of Snip 'n' Curl, in the middle of the mall.

"See you in a couple hours," she says. "Good luck."

Meriel takes me to the sinks in the back, obviously eager to finally get started.

After washing my hair, she sits me down at her station and combs out the tangles. "Basically, do you want to keep it long? Or do you want a real drastic change?"

I'm opposed to drastic change on principle. I'm much more in favor of blending in. While I'm hesitating, I hear one of the other customers laughing, and my heart feels ready to explode because for a second I think Alison has come in while I was getting my hair washed. I start to get up to go over and tell her how happy I am she's here. But then I think, *What if she's so angry at me that she slaps me? Right here in front of everyone?*

But it's only the girl who came in after me. She's an attractive brunette who looks absolutely nothing like Alison.

"Hold on," I tell Meriel. I get my purse from under my chair, and I pull out the picture of Alison. "Can you give me a perm that will make me look like this?" I ask.

"Sure," Meriel tells me. "I'll use the biggest size rollers and give you a gentle body perm."

I take a deep breath. "OK," I say.

24

Meriel tells me that Alison is beautiful and asks whether she's my sister, though she sounds amazed at the idea that the two of us could have emerged from the same gene pool. It reminds me of Ms. LaMond fussing over the same picture a few days ago.

As I sit there, with Meriel covering my head with rollers that don't look all that big to me, I start thinking about Alison, and Ms. LaMond, and the art contest that Ms. LaMond wants Alison to enter. As Meriel squirts a totally foul-smelling substance all over my head—a substance that pricks my nose and stings my eyes—I think back to another of Ms. LaMond's art projects and how badly that turned out.

This was back when Ms. LaMond was Miss LaMond. It was her final gift to Alison's eighth-grade class—a parting shot before marrying Mr. Van Strydonk and heading off for parts unknown. It probably made sense to her. She'd had the class make little flower baskets to present to their mothers on Mother's Day. The least she could do for the fathers was to have the kids make Father's Day cards. How was she supposed to keep up on which kids didn't have fathers?

That was the year I was in third grade—which, unlike Alison, I most emphatically was not in danger of skipping—and I was very much into ballet. Ah, the ballet phase. Our bathroom—then as now—was the only room that had a full-length mirror, so I spent a lot of my time in there, practicing my steps.

I remember the day; I remember Alison bursting in without knocking.

"Third position," I said, ignoring her. "Fourth position. Fifth." I held onto the towel rack and started doing pliés.

"Can I borrow your backpack?" Alison asked.

I was surprised, but I didn't lose count. "I thought backpacks were for kids," I said, because Alison always sneered at me for being younger. "What happened to carrying your books in your arms like the other eighth graders?"

"Never mind," she said. "Can I use it?"

I slung my leg across the corner of the sink and started my stretches. "Sure. But my stuff is going to be in there, too. You think you can carry all that?"

"No," she said, "because I want to use it today. Now."

I glanced over at her without releasing my ankle. "You are aware, of course, that today is Saturday."

"Don't try to talk like Wally," Alison snapped. "It sounds

stupid from him and even worse from you." Wally and Mom had been married for about six months, and we were still hoping Mom would come to her senses and divorce him and remarry Dad. Or that Wally would catch some awful disease and die. And Mom would remarry Dad.

In any case, sarcastic disdain sounded more like Alison than Wally.

I shrugged at Alison and switched legs.

"Well?" she asked impatiently.

"Where do you want to take it?"

She didn't answer.

"You better tell me," I said, "because I'm going with you. I'm not letting you take it out of my sight." You'd think there wouldn't be that many things a nine-year-old could have that a thirteen-year-old would be interested in, but Alison had practiced her hairdressing skills on several of my Barbies, and she'd lost or ruined more of my hair bows and barrettes than *I* had.

"Come on, Susan," she wheedled.

"I let you take my baton to Megan's house," I said, reminding her of her latest destruction of my goods, "and it came back with one of the tips gone."

"That was last year," Alison said. Considering that this was early June, December wasn't as far back as she was trying to make it sound. "And it was Megan's fault," she added.

"You're standing in front of the mirror," I said, rising onto my toes.

"Please."

It was nice to have Alison be the one doing the begging for a change. "What do you need it for?" I asked.

Alison sighed. "I have to carry something."

"Ah! That explains everything! Thank you very much!" Third grade wasn't only my year for ballet; it was my year for sarcasm.

Alison said, "You're talking like *him* again."

I studied my face in the mirror and sucked in my cheeks, trying even back then to attain the look that comes to Sigrid so effortlessly. I pulled my hair into a bun on top of my head.

"You're rotten," Alison said. Then she lowered her voice. "I want to buy a present for Father's Day tomorrow, to go with my card, and the bag will make it easier to carry everything."

I let my hair drop. I didn't know how to pin it up anyway. Besides, ballerinas don't wear glasses. "You're getting a present for Wally?" I asked in amazement.

She gave me a disgusted look. "Is old Weasel Eyes our father?"

I'm not sure that at nine I had ever seen a weasel, much less noticed its eyes, and I doubt that Alison had either. But she had heard the phrase somewhere and loved to use it.

"You mean Daddy?" I asked. This was before Dad moved to California. He still lived in Port Champlain, but Port Champlain is a big place. "We don't even know where he lives now," I said.

Alison wiggled her eyebrows at me. "Oh, no?"

"What have you been up to?" I asked.

"I looked through Mom's things," she said with a matter-of-factness that was dizzying. "You didn't think I was going to waste that beautiful card I made in art class on that big clod *Wally*?"

I'd seen the card and it *was* beautiful, but what I was thinking was that Wally wasn't all that bad. But from the first time we had met him, Alison had insisted his most endearing quality was the fact that he owned a pickup truck. And since he said it was too dangerous for us to ride in the back, it didn't amount to much. Wally had never beaten us or left us out in the woods like fairy-tale stepfathers, but after all, Daddy was still Daddy.

"It'll only take me a couple seconds to change out of my tights," I said. Then, never suspecting what I was starting, I added, "I can make a card, too. In fact I have an idea for one already."

Alison followed me into my room. "Nobody invited you, you little wretch."

"But you *did* invite my backpack," I reminded her.

She made a face.

"What did you get for Daddy?" I asked, pulling all of my clothes out of the drawers. After all, I hadn't seen him in almost two years, and I wanted to make a good impression.

"I haven't gotten anything yet. We've got to go downtown and choose something."

"Downtown?" I said. "You mean we're going to take a bus by ourselves and go downtown?"

"*You* don't have to if you don't want to," Alison sneered. "Besides, what did you think—that Daddy lives over on the next block? We have to pass through downtown anyway."

I gulped, but didn't ask any more questions for fear of bringing more of Alison's scorn down on me. The older we got, the less we got along, but still Alison was the picture of everything I wanted to be: beautiful and talented and self-assured.

After finally settling on the third pair of shorts I tried on, and the fifth shirt, I sat down with glue, scissors, my *Living Ballet* book, and construction paper. Accompanied by Alison's loud and frequent sighs, I made a card for the father who had left four years earlier and who had visited less and less frequently since then.

Thinking about this, I decided to try one more question. "What if he doesn't want to see us?" I asked with studied casualness. "After all, he's never called or anything."

"Of course he has," Alison snorted. "He's called; he's written; he's tried to visit. But old Weasel Eyes won't let him in, and he won't tell us about the letters and calls."

Gullible as I was back in third grade, that was a bit much, even for me. I looked up from the project I was gluing together and found Alison's expression daring me to disagree. I didn't.

25

Mom spied us on the way out.

"Susan and I are going to Megan's to study for our exams," Alison called, and Mom barely looked up from her ironing to wave. "Dinner at five-thirty," she reminded us. Which gave us two and a half hours. The exams Alison and Megan were studying for were five years ahead of the ones I'd be taking, but apparently that fact either didn't cross Mom's mind or didn't bother her.

We walked past Megan's and waited at the bus stop. I could hardly keep still; this was all so exciting. Alison looked down her nose at me and said, "Kids! I hope you don't do anything to embarrass me."

I went into my pirouettes, moves for which the bathroom was too small. Alison turned her back on me and pretended we weren't together.

Once the bus came, the trip took longer than I had imagined.

But it didn't take as long as the search for just the right present for our father.

"I thought you had something planned," I grumbled.

"I haven't seen him in a while either!" she cried. "I'm not hearing any brilliant suggestions from you."

I hadn't seen her so tense in a long time: this was her year for cool disdain.

Downtown was huge. There were so many stores, and many of them had several floors. In our neighborhood there was a florist, a jewelry store, a drugstore, and Carrol's—sort of a discount everything store. I had thought these offered endless possibilities when I had broken into my piggy bank the previous month to get a Mother's Day present.

"We're going to spend all our time here and not have time to see Daddy," I warned, perhaps whining just a bit.

Alison smacked my arm, but I lucked out because something attracted her attention. She pointed to a big sign that said FATHER'S DAY: GIFTS FOR THAT SPECIAL MAN.

Alison and I went up to the counter.

There were ties and cuff links and belts and pen sets, and stuff we, or at least I, couldn't even identify.

I gulped at the prices. "How much money have you got?" I whispered to Alison.

She opened her wallet. "Did you bring any?" she asked.

I dug into my pocket and pulled out what I had. Hasty addition made us realize that the two of us together couldn't afford most of what was in the display case.

"We should have gotten something at Carrol's," I hissed.

"Carrol's doesn't have anything good enough for Daddy," Alison shot back.

A store clerk, an incredibly tall lady wearing a lot of make-up, cleared her throat. "Girls, I couldn't help but overhear," she said, and I thought I was going to die of embarrassment. But she was smiling in a friendly manner. "Maybe if you showed me what you have to spend, I could help you choose."

I half expected her to laugh at how poor we were, but she didn't. "How about a nice cologne?" she suggested. She brought us to where there were all different kinds and opened the test bottles for us to sniff.

"That's the kind Wally uses," I said at a familiar lemon-lime scent.

Alison groaned. "Oh, really! Sometimes I think you like the man."

The clerk's attention was momentarily diverted by another customer, and I took the opportunity to say, "He's all right."

"He's all right," she mimicked. "You'd say that about anybody who was willing to pay for your dumb ballet lessons."

"Well?" I said.

"Well, he's just trying to buy your affection."

"You let him buy you that Walkman."

Alison kicked my foot. "Well, then, spend your money on Weasel Eyes if you want to."

"I don't," I protested. "I want to buy something for Daddy. I want Daddy to be happy to see us. I want him to come home with us to stay forever." I was always an easy crier.

Alison rolled her eyes. "Don't start in on me!" she said between clenched teeth. She pulled out a ratty-looking handkerchief and shoved it into my face. "Hurry up," she said. "The saleslady's coming back."

The tall saleslady smiled down at us. "Have you girls decided on one?" she asked.

"How about this?" Alison pointed at a set that included a bar of shaving soap, a little mug and brush, and after-shave lotion.

The price—once tax was added—almost wiped out our total savings. But the saleslady wrapped it in silver paper and tied a fancy bow on it. We put the package in my backpack so that we wouldn't get the paper all fingerprinty, and we went back out to wait for the bus to Daddy's place.

Which was when Alison broke the news to me.

"I hope you can convince the driver that you're six," she said, "because we don't have enough money left for both of us."

"How'll we get back?" I squealed.

"Daddy'll drive us," Alison said confidently.

I glared at her.

"Or maybe he'll pay for a taxi."

Somehow, I refrained from kicking her.

"Or at least he'll give us bus fare." She grinned. "Don't worry about it. Everything is under control. *If* you can convince the bus driver you're six."

I didn't worry about it—not because I trusted that everything would work out, but because the bus came then and I had to scrunch down small and concentrate on looking six.

I was sure we'd be hauled off and arrested, but the driver didn't even glance at me, which is a good thing, because I must have looked like a nine-year-old hunchback with mental problems. We sat in the back and I asked Alison if she knew where we had to get off.

"Are you kidding?" she asked. "I'm not even sure this is the right bus line. That's a joke," she assured me quickly. "Relax."

Yeah, right.

26

The bus made several turns, and we kept watching the street signs until we were on Columbus Avenue and Alison said, "This is it! Now we're looking for number 3647."

We ended up passing the building before we knew it, and even after we pulled the cord, the bus kept going for another block.

Number 3647 was a small apartment building. We went in through the front door and saw four mailboxes. Three were labeled, but none of them said "Casselman."

We went up a flight of stairs to apartment C, the one whose mailbox didn't have any name, and Alison knocked.

A woman opened the door.

When Alison and I were younger and had gotten along well enough to talk to each other, we had woven fantasies about Daddy coming back to get us. He and Mom would make up whatever it was that had caused them to fight, and we'd all move back into our old house. Wally's coming had made that seem less likely—though possible if we drove Wally off or if he died—but it had never occurred to me that Daddy as well as Mom could have remarried. One look at Alison's face assured me that she was equally surprised.

Alison recovered herself first. "Is our father here?"

The woman looked vaguely amused, though by no means friendly. "I don't think so, kid," she said, and started to shut the door.

"I'm Alison. This is Susan."

The woman was getting more annoyed with each moment of her time that we took. "Jake!" she yelled into the apartment. "There're two kids out here looking for their father. You know anything about that?"

There was a mumbled reply from inside the apartment, and the woman said to us, "Satisfied?"

We were—even without hearing the answer: Daddy's name is Stephen, not Jake.

Alison and I left the building and waited outside for the woman in apartment C to close her door before we reentered.

Alison knocked on one of the first-floor doors, the one with the mailbox labeled "Valez."

A man we didn't know answered.

"We're looking for Stephen Casselman," Alison said.

The man looked behind him, then stepped back into the apartment as another man came out.

"Yeah?" this second man said.

"Daddy?" I asked.

My father narrowed his eyes at me. "Alison?"

"Susan," I corrected. *Nobody* else—before or since—has ever gotten the two of us confused. "That's Alison."

"Good Lord," he said. "Little Susan and Alison. Good Lord."

Somehow, I smiled at him. If he was shocked by how we had changed, the feeling was mutual. I remembered him mostly from the stories Alison had told, and from pictures. He had seemed a tall, slender, handsome prince, like the one in *Swan Lake,* with blond curly hair and lips always curved up in a smile. He was still tall, but the hair had darkened and thinned. I couldn't see much of his mouth because of his beard. "Good Lord," he repeated, looking from me to Alison to me to Alison.

"We came to visit you," Alison explained in an uncharacteristically small voice. "For Father's Day."

"Father's Day. Oh, yeah. Ahm . . . Shouldn't you be in school or something?"

Alison and I glanced at each other. "It's Saturday," I said.

"It's five o'clock," she said.

"Good Lord," he said.

We all looked at each other some more. The door to apartment C opened, and a large man came and looked over the railing, his tee shirt clinging to his sweating belly.

Daddy glanced at him distastefully and motioned for us to come in.

"Hey," we heard the man calling behind us. "They belong to *Miss* Casselman downstairs."

The door shut off his wife's reply, but I felt Alison stiffen next to me. I was too young and excited to give any thought to anything besides Daddy.

Daddy led us into the kitchen.

"My daughters, Alison and Susan," Daddy explained to his friend, the man who had opened the door. Daddy didn't introduce us to him, but I figured he must be Valez. It wasn't until a couple years later that I learned his first name—Hector. "They're here for Father's Day," Daddy told Hector.

We all smiled at each other, except for Alison, who seemed to be going into one of her sulks.

"Lemonade?" Hector offered.

I was so hot and thirsty from the ride, I immediately took a drink. But he must have just made it: it was still lukewarm. There was too much water and sugar and not enough lemon. I put the glass back down.

Alison hadn't touched hers. She just kept looking from Daddy to Hector in the same disbelieving way that Daddy kept looking from her to me.

"Well, well," he said. After a pause, he said it again. Then: "So. What exactly brings you?"

"We came to see you," I said, since Alison didn't seem to be saying anything. "For Father's Day."

"Right," he said.

"We brought a present for you." I had already opened the

backpack and taken out the silver-wrapped package before I thought of the beard. "Oh."

"What?" Daddy asked.

"It's shaving stuff."

Now it was his turn to say it: "Oh." He turned the package over and over without opening it.

"But we have cards for you," I said brightly.

"Oh," he said again. "How nice."

"Come on, Alison," I said to get her involved in all this, because her hanging back was becoming obvious. "Give him your card first." I held out the backpack to her.

"I think I lost it on the way," she said sullenly, which I knew wasn't true. It was in the backpack, to keep it from getting crunched.

But Daddy had already said "Oh" again, and I didn't want to call Alison a liar, since she obviously didn't want to give Daddy the card.

"Well, I still have mine." I reached into the backpack again. "It's not as nice as Alison's, but I made it myself." I handed him the construction paper, which still felt kind of yucky from the globs of not-quite-dried paste. I nervously gulped more of the lemonade and wiped my sweaty palms on my shorts as Daddy stared at my card.

"This is just dandy," our father said. "Real nice." He held it out for Hector to see. Hector beamed at me. Daddy looked at the card again, and I could see that he was puzzled though he didn't say so. I had cut the picture out from one of my ballet books. It had ruined the section on *The Nutcracker Suite,* but as soon as I had thought of it, I knew no other card would do.

But maybe he wasn't familiar with the ballet. "That's from the Dance of the Sugarplum Fairy," I explained.

"Sugarplum . . . ?"

I couldn't understand his not understanding. "Sugarplum Fairy." Still nothing. "Since that's what Mom always calls you." His jaw dropped at that. "I thought it was some sort of love name," I said lamely.

Alison gasped.

Daddy turned several shades of purple.

Hector choked on his lemonade.

"Get out!" Daddy yelped. "That's it! You're just like your mother! Did she send you? Never mind, don't answer, just get out." He shoved the present and the card at me. I was barely able to snatch up my backpack as he practically pushed us out the door. Just as previously I'd been sure he'd eventually come back, now I was sure he hated us. And it was all my fault.

Out on the street, I looked at Alison. "Oh, Alison," I said, beginning to cry.

She ignored the tears on her own cheeks. "Boy, are you ever nai-ive," she said.

27

The fact that my father is gay and has a live-in lover named Hector isn't something I'm especially pleased about; I don't go around telling people.

Connie knows, of course. Back in third grade she was already my best friend. When I told her what had happened, I was amazed that she wasn't surprised, and she admitted that her parents and her older sister had already guessed. She hadn't said anything to me because nobody was sure, and she thought it was an awful thing to say if it *weren't* true.

The only other person I've told is Wakisha, who I only met this year, but she's not the kind of person who talks about you behind your back. She said it was no big deal, that God created families to be an embarrassment, and that she has an uncle who plays in a professional polka band.

The thing that really upset me about that disastrous visit with Daddy was the way he acted as though he didn't especially like us—even before I accidentally insulted him—the way he seemed embarrassed by us and eager to get us out of there.

A couple years later he came to visit, to let us know that he and Hector were moving. Hector is a lifeguard, which in upstate New York is a very part-time job, and Dad is really good with computers, so they decided to move to California. Dad and I went for a walk around the block and had a long talk. He said that he *had* been embarrassed that day—not of us, but because he didn't want us to know about him and Hector because he thought we were too young; he was taken by surprise by our sudden visit and how grown-up we looked. I told him that I should have used the picture of the prince from *Swan Lake,* and we've gotten along fine ever since.

Alison, however, never forgave him.

Her friends *had* told her what the rumors were about him, and she had told them they were wrong and stupid. Once she found out *she* was wrong, she was furious that she had defended him. She was sure that people would assume that a gay parent would have gay kids and that people were talking about her.

I'm not sure she ever recovered from that day.

By the time we got home, it was almost seven o'clock.

We had used the last of our money to get to Daddy's apartment and certainly hadn't dared go back to ask him for a loan for bus fare. We walked all the way downtown, following the bus stop signs. Once there, we threw ourselves on the mercy of the salesclerk who had helped us earlier.

Alison asked her to take back the shaving kit in exchange

for bus fare—but of course we didn't tell her why. The woman told us to keep our father's present and went into her own purse to give us enough money so that we could get home. She also gave us a lecture on better planning.

We got off the bus at our street and immediately spotted Wally's pickup truck cruising around.

And Wally spotted us.

He pulled up next to us and leaned over to open the door. Alison and I jostled each other for better position. I lost and got in next to him.

From where I sat, I got a better view of him than Alison did. Dumb as I was when I was nine (and Alison frequently reminded me that I was *very* dumb), I knew by the stiff way he sat and by his grip on the steering wheel that I didn't want to be the one to break the silence.

Nobody said anything until we reached home.

The table was set, but nobody had eaten; the pots and pans were still on the stove, filled with food.

Alison took all this in, then asked, casually and innocently, "Where's Mom?"

"Where the hell have you been?" Wally screamed.

We both cringed. "We're sorry," I offered.

"Do you have any idea how worried we were when we found out you'd never made it to Megan's?" I don't think Wally had ever yelled at us before, but he was making up for lost time. "Your mother's out checking the neighbors one by one," he yelled at us. "She's convinced you had to be lying dead in some dark alley."

We didn't answer, and after a few seconds he went to the phone. At first I thought he was trying to locate Mom, but then I realized he was talking to the police, telling them to call off the search, we'd been found. A few phone calls later, he was able to reach Mom and tell her we were safe.

That done, he turned back to us. "Have you eaten?" he asked. Very stiff. Very formal. Never looking directly at us.

"No," we mumbled, and he turned the stove on to reheat the dinner, which had been abandoned.

With a sigh, he sat down at the table and rubbed one of his large hands across his face. He pushed his glasses up onto his forehead and left his hand there.

"Was she angry?" Alison asked.

"No," Wally said. "Relieved."

There was something about his voice . . .

Alison and I looked at each other incredulously. She took a step closer to him. "Are you *crying*?" she asked softly. And, even more amazed, "Over *us*?"

He turned slightly before taking down his hand, as if that would keep us from seeing the tears. Then he got up and found something to busy himself with at the stove.

I ran to give him a hug from behind, and it was a good thing he's such a big guy or I would have knocked him into the stroganoff, he was so unprepared.

Then Alison did something that I never asked her about. But—for self-preservation or out of true affection—she reached into my backpack and pulled out the gift-wrapped box. "We got this for you," she said. "Happy Father's Day."

Wally looked at both of us in disbelief for a couple seconds, then he swept us both up into a bear hug. "My dear little girls," he whispered.

Alison, her face pressed simultaneously against both of ours, whispered back, "Dear Wally."

But she never did give him the card.

28

At the Snip 'n Curl, Meriel the hairdresser finally decides that she's tortured me enough.

Just as I feel that I'm about to pass out from the fumes of the perm solution, she squirts something else all over my head that she says is neutralizer. It feels cold and itchy as it drips all over my scalp. Meriel has put these wads of cotton that look like tampons all over the edge of my hairline to keep the various solutions from running into my face or down my back, but I keep feeling those individual drips working their way down and I'm certain one of them is going to make it through the cotton.

Finally—slowly, methodically—she removes the rollers. I'm feeling real claustrophobic and want to just rip them out and get out of here, but Meriel wants to make sure I'm convinced Mom and I are getting our money's worth.

Once the rollers are out, I look like Shirley Temple, but that isn't the end of it. Meriel uses a blow dryer to get rid of every bit of curl, so that my hair sticks out perfectly straight in all directions. I look like an untamed cone of cotton candy. Finally she uses the curling iron to give me a hairstyle that seems to belong on a country and western singer. I feel that I should have rhinestones, cowboy boots, and a broken heart. I don't have to worry that my mother will recognize Alison's hair on me. My hair looks almost exactly the opposite of Alison's.

"What do you think, hon?" Meriel asks. All the other hairdressers swarm over to say how wonderful I look. I figure I look like walking hair, with a small body attached for mobility's sake. Could this possibly be the look Matt Burke has been waiting to see on me?

"It's a little bit high here," I say, indicating on top.

The other hairdressers insist it looks fine while Meriel presses down on the top with her hands. It springs right back up to exactly where it was before, and Meriel says, "There! That's better!"

I don't want to start an argument. I figure the haircut and the perm are the important things. I can style it myself.

Mom's returned while my back has been to the door, and she comes over and says my hair looks nice. She's my mother—what else can she say?

"Happy?" she asks me.

"Ecstatic," I tell her. I just want to get in the fresh air so I can breathe again.

But the fresh air doesn't help; I'm carrying the stink with me.

As soon as we get home, I wash my hair, several times, until the smell is gone.

I'm hoping that if I don't blow-dry it, the curling iron will make the hair look more natural, like Alison's. It takes forever to dry, and I still look like Shirley Temple. On a bad day.

Sunday I experiment all day with my hair. I wash it again and try to style it while blow-drying, but it still comes out looking witchy. I use the curling iron, which takes forever and curls my hair in all the wrong places.

Each time I come out of the bathroom, Mom and Wally tell me I look fine. Bryan just rolls around on the floor, shrieking with laughter, but he's quick enough to get away when I try to catch him.

Maybe, I think, I've overworked my hair, so I wash it again.

Between working with my hair, I polish my fingernails to enhance my new sophisticated look, but none of the colors satisfy me either—which I recognize to be a result of a growing crankiness because of my hair. I end up taking the polish off, leaving a pinkish residue on the skin around my nails.

Dad calls again. Twice in two weeks is more than usual. I wonder if he's calling back to talk to me because Mom has called him and told him I'm depressed about my hair.

But Dad doesn't mention my hair at all. He says, "I'm coming to Port Champlain the last week of October."

"Great," I say, honestly pleased, because he doesn't make it back here very often. "Any special reason?"

"Do I need a special reason to see my little girl?" he asks brightly, which is no answer at all.

"No," I tell him, trying to keep the suspicion out of my voice. "Does Mom know you're coming?"

"Of course she knows." Again, that bright, bright brightness.

"Well, good," I force myself to say because I have to say something. I'm looking across the room to where Mom's sitting on the couch, a book in her hand as though she's reading, but she's looking at me with a smile as bright as Dad's voice.

Of course she knows.

I can just imagine.

After I get off the phone, I try Mom's electric rollers.

I tell Mom I want to sue Meriel, but she thinks I'm joking and laughs.

29

I decide that maybe the problem is that blow-drying my hair is getting it too wild to control. Monday morning I decide to let my hair air dry before I use the heated rollers.

But I've forgotten how very long it now takes to dry. I take my shower before Bryan, and I keep thinking that my hair is dry. But every time I poke into it, it's still wet underneath.

Finally, I use the rollers anyway—the instructions say they can be used while the hair is still damp—but as I'm taking them out, I can feel that it's still damp, and as soon as I brush my hair, all the curl goes out and the frizz comes in.

I set my hair a second time, and that seems to mostly finish off the job of drying it, but it still comes out frizzy, especially near where the hair attaches to my head.

Mom is yelling at me that it's getting late, and I don't have time to reset *all* my hair, so I just do it for a third time on top and in front.

At this point, it doesn't actually look bad. It doesn't look like Alison's hair, but then Matt Burke has never seen Alison to compare us, thank God. All in all, I'm pleased.

Despite the fact that I got up at five and the bus comes at a quarter after seven, I don't have time to eat, though my mother tells me she's put a banana in my jacket pocket. At least I'm grateful for the warning. You don't want to be reaching into your pocket and finding a banana when you aren't expecting one.

It's raining as I run from the front door to the bus. I plunk myself down in a window seat and check my reflection. I give myself a damp grin.

As close as Connie lives, she takes a different bus, so she's going to have to wait till lunch to see me—unless we run into each other in the hall, a meeting that is too short to be fun when someone wants to show off a new hairstyle or piece of jewelry or—on the rare dress-up or dress-down days—new clothes.

The bus goes around the neighborhood, picking up girls on their way to Mother of Sorrows and boys heading for Cardinal O'Gorman. A boy with a wool coat sits next to me, smelling like a herd of wet sheep. The windshield wipers screech and thump across the windshield.

I steal another glance in the window and am alarmed to see that my hair has grown—not longer, but more volume, from the humidity. I consider asking the wet kid next to me to move, before his dampness seeps into my hair, but I decide he's not likely to budge anyway.

By the time I make it indoors, my hair's doing its Bride of Frankenstein impression.

"Nice hair," Melissa Prawel sneers. "Stick your finger in an electrical socket?"

Even Robin Liccardi can't find anything nice to say.

I see Wakisha's eyes widen in amazement, and I sit down and lay my head on my desk, wondering if I can convince Mr. Rosenblum that I have the flu and need to be sent home. Of course that would mean calling Mom or Wally at work to pick me up. Considering what they saw me going through with my hair yesterday, they're not likely to believe I'm really sick unless I can manage to produce a 105-degree fever or projectile vomiting.

I'm aware of Wakisha sitting down at Gail Kraynik's desk across the aisle from me. "You OK, Sibyl?" she asks.

"I've got hair flu," I tell her.

Wakisha says, "Last time I saw hair that big was when my aunt tried some home straightening formula she ordered through a TV ad."

"Did it eventually get better?" I ask.

"Sure," Wakisha says, "after she cut it off."

I hear Bertie Dunbar's voice. "What did you *do*?" she asks.

"I got a perm," I admit. "I haven't learned to work with it yet."

"What do you mean?" Robin asks.

Still without raising my head from the desk, I say, "Well, I washed it and set it a whole bunch of times, but I'm not sure what's the best approach."

There're a few seconds of silence. Total silence. I lift my head. "What?" I say.

"When did you get this perm?" Joanne Tramonto asks in a very significant tone.

The scary thing is, I don't know *why* that question should be significant.

"Saturday," I tell them.

"And you fiddled with it already today?" Bertie asks.

"I *fiddled* with it Saturday," I say. "I washed *and* set it."

Everybody groans. Everybody.

Joanne says, "When *I* get a perm, they tell me nothing smaller than my elbow is supposed to touch my hair for three days. No rollers or curling iron. No finger arranging, even. You aren't supposed to wash your hair for a week."

I put my head back down on the desk and say, "I think my hair flu just went down to my stomach."

Wakisha goes to her own desk ahead of mine, but then asks Mary Amber DeFranco, behind me, to move. Mary Amber sighs, to let everyone know what an inconvenience we are and how kind she is to put up with us without complaining, and then she moves.

"Sit up," Wakisha orders.

She's got a big comb and a ponytail elastic and industrial-strength hair-slicking gunk.

Mr. Rosenblum comes in during the middle of this opera-tion. Usually he tells us that hairstyling and make-up are to be done in the ladies' rooms, not the classrooms, but obviously he can see that this is an emergency, and he ignores us.

Wakisha pulls my hair back real tight away from my face and into a french braid every bit as classy as Mrs. Fallahi's Evangeline's, except she's used enough styling gel to make my hair look plastic.

I check it out in the mirror from my purse. "Thank you," I say. Anything's better, and this really isn't bad at all. "But will it stay?"

Robin donates a can of hair spray, and Wakisha uses half of it on me.

Sitting at his desk, Rosenblum begins to choke and wave his arms. "Is all that really necessary?" he asks.

"Yes," three-quarters of the class answers in unison.

30

My hair and I make it through the day without major mishap. At lunch, Connie sympathizes but does indicate it's all my fault: if I had talked it over with her before taking such a drastic step, or if I had answered her calls Sunday afternoon, this wouldn't have happened.

At rehearsal, Matt keeps looking at me with that frozen kind of expression like people wear when they can't tear their gaze from a car accident.

"Maybe," Connie whispers to me, "today wouldn't be the best day to invite him to the dance."

"OK," I tell her.

Wakisha has applied so much gel and hair spray that I'm wondering if—should some other dancer bump into me—my hair would shatter.

Naturally, the day I'm eager to get out of there, rehearsal

runs later than usual. Mrs. Miraglia, who usually picks us up by the back door, finally comes in to see what's keeping us. Several of the other parents are there, too, giving Father Kevin dark looks until he finally calls a stop.

Mom is not pleased about my being more than a half-hour late. She says I should have called.

I point out that most likely Father Kevin would have objected to my leaving the stage during the actual practice, and that finding a phone afterward probably would have taken longer than having Mrs. Miraglia drive us.

Mom says if I start getting smart, I can just forget about the play entirely.

I say that she's been looking for an excuse to back out of letting me be in the play anyway.

She looks about to take back her permission right then and there, but Wally steps in. "Nobody should make decisions in the heat of being hungry and angry," he says.

Mom glares at me but doesn't say anything, and Wally tells me that nobody appreciates a smart aleck.

"I am *so* glad her father is coming next week," Mom tells Wally as though I'm not standing right there to hear. Mom has never before shown any inclination to look forward to Dad's visits.

"What?" I ask. I'm trying very hard not to use anything near what Mom could call That Tone, but she can spot That Tone in the most innocent of my statements. Alison could get away with *anything* compared to me.

And, sure enough: "Don't you take That Tone with me, young lady," Mom warns.

"All I'm doing is asking what Daddy has to do with anything," I point out in a perfectly reasonable way. How come *I'm* always the one who has to be reasonable around here? Why isn't that a standard for anyone else?

"We're all going to the psychologist together," Mom says. "The whole family."

Dad's coming across the continent for an appointment with a psychologist? What has Mom been telling him?

"I told you the guidance counselors have to fill their quotas," I protest. "How's Mrs. Owen going to keep her job if nobody talks to her?"

Mom just looks at me.

I try to think of a brilliant comeback, but all I can dredge up is, "Well, I'm going to my room."

After a long, quiet dinner, I wash my hair again and let it air dry. I no longer look quite as good as Shirley Temple. My hair is simultaneously limp and kinky and bushy and flat. I look the way Shirley Temple might have if she had ever drowned. Or Wakisha is right: I look like a black woman who's made a serious mistake.

Mom comes in just as I'm crying, and that makes her feel so bad about yelling at me earlier that she says I can stay in the play, but I absolutely must tell Father Kevin I have to leave on time, *or* I have to let her know if I'm going to be late. I tell her what I learned about perms—that they're not to be washed or rearranged—and she's all for bringing me back to Snip 'n' Curl to see if they can fix me up again.

"No," I say, remembering that country and western hairstyle Meriel gave me. "I'll work with what I've got. It's got to get better with practice."

But I know it never will.

31

The next day is one of our phys. ed. days, and somebody gives Coach Merenda a hard time about something or other, and somebody else laughs, and the next thing we know she has us running up and down four flights of stairs twenty-five times.

My hair starts to grow.

They have showers at Mother of Sorrows, but I have no idea why—unless they're for the afterschool jocks—because Coach Merenda never has us use them. This has never been a problem before, because I have a policy of never raising a sweat in phys. ed. On this particular day, however, there are twenty-five girls in the ladies' room, washing our faces in the sinks and splashing water on our armpits so that we won't cause our classmates to pass out when we enter our afternoon classes. The cramped accommodations being what they are—and the rest of us being ticked off at the two who smart-mouthed Merenda—the ladies' room ends up quite wet, and my hair grows some more.

By the time I make it to Cardinal O'Gorman for rehearsal, my hair looks like Michael Jackson's did in the 1970s.

An hour of hectic dancing doesn't help.

During our break, Connie forces me to sit down next to Matt Burke, even though it's obvious that Matt is busy trying to get a conversation going with Sigrid. When Matt glances in our direction to answer Connie's insistent "Hi," Sigrid says "Excuse me" and slips away. Connie has the sense not to say to Matt, "Look at Sibyl's new hair. Doesn't it look nice?" Connie has the sense not to say anything.

We sit there on the edge of the table, silently drinking from our bottles of pop, Matt sulking because Sigrid is gone, Connie and I sulking because Matt is ignoring me.

I've taken my glasses off—which I do every break—so I can hardly see a thing, but somebody walks by, and then Mary Amber DeFranco's voice calls out to me. Now, she's seen me all day, but she picks this moment to ask, "Was Sister Beatrice using your hair to do experiments in static electricity today?"

Being real quick on my feet with sarcastic comebacks, I say, "Uh, no."

Connie says, real loud as Mary Amber is walking away, "Don't pay any attention to her. She went to K-mart for a liposuction procedure, and they accidentally sucked her brain out through her belly button."

I think that's a pretty good rebuttal and turn to Matt to see if he's as amused as I am.

Matt, on the other hand, has finally taken notice of my hair. He's looking at me with this expression of part shock part wonder, and part disbelief. We're sitting close enough that I have no trouble at all making any of this out.

We're also sitting close enough that I'm beginning to notice a peculiar smell. Matt might be drinking from a bottle marked GINGER ALE, but it sure doesn't smell like ginger ale. *He's got beer in there,* I realize.

Mary Amber is calling back to Connie, "You need a personality transplant," and Connie retaliates, "You need a personality," and all this while Matt *still* hasn't taken his eyes off my hair or said a word.

"Mary Amber's a vicious little ferret," Connie says. "Don't you think so, Matt?"

Matt says nothing.

"*I* think Sibyl's hair is cute," Connie says.

Matt says nothing.

"*Matt,*" Connie says sharply. If we were in a World War II movie, she'd slap him in the face and tell him, "Snap out of it."

Matt's gaze finally diverts to Connie. The daze is beginning to dissipate. All in all, I'm still putting his lack of connection down to what he's been drinking. "Yeah," he says. But then his eyes are drawn back to me again.

"Excuse me," I say. Maybe I can find a spare razor somewhere, and just shave every bit of hair off my head.

I go back toward the auditorium and nearly run down Spencer Pabrinkis, the guy in charge of the lights.

He reels back from me and says, "Your hair!"

I'm about to tell him to shut up, when he says, "I love it!"

129

He might be trying to be kind, or he might be being sarcastic, so I don't dare say anything.

He says, "You must be really pleased with it."

"It . . ." I say, ". . . is taking some getting used to."

"I love hair with an attitude!" Spencer says.

With his hair, I guess he'd pretty much have to.

Connie comes running up to me. "Are you OK?" she demands. I can see, rather than feel, her touching my hair. "Do you want me to try to fix it like Wakisha did?"

"No," I say. Spencer has a tendency to melt away whenever there's more than two people around, and he's already heading backstage. "No," I repeat, "I'm OK."

The rehearsal runs long again. As soon as Father Kevin lets us leave the stage, I make a mad dash for the pay phone.

Mom is only slightly furious.

When we get home, I learn that, by being on the phone, I missed all the excitement.

Mrs. Miraglia comes in to talk to Mom. She tells her that she and all the other parents who have spent the last two evenings waiting out in the parking lot for twenty to thirty extra minutes ganged up on Father Kevin and demanded better timekeeping on his part. In response, Father Kevin has officially lengthened rehearsals, so that now, instead of running from three to five, they will go from three to five-thirty, but he promises dismissal will be prompt.

While I'm sure that if *I* came home with this story, Mom would have said, "Do you expect the whole family to dela dinner just for you?" now she looks at Mrs. Miraglia and asks, "Is that still all right for you for picking up the girls?"

"Certainly," Mrs. Miraglia says.

Then Mom gives a then-who-am-I-to-stand-in-the-way-of-art? smile and says, "Thank you. I guess that will work out for us, too."

32

Eventually I notice that—depending on the day's humidity—usually my hair looks better in the evening than it does in the morning. I finally succumb to the advice that Wally and my dad have been trying to push on me all year and start taking my showers in the evening. Bryan can live in the tub come morning as far as I'm concerned.

And one day Matt Burke comes up to me—spontaneously, as far as I know, though Connie *may* have put him up to it—and tells me that my hair looks nice.

I've had a long time to prepare for this, and I say, "Uh . . . thanks."

33

The day after my father arrives from California, all five of us go to the psychologist: me, Dad, Mom, Wally, and Bryan. The psychologist, whose name is Dr. Meagher, has teeth that are too short and small—he looks like either he files them down or he's never lost his baby teeth. I decide immediately to hate him.

The first thing he says, as soon as we're all sitting down, is that we all need to stand up.

"I hope he isn't going to have us do exercises," I mumble to whoever is listening, which I don't think is anyone. I'm trembling, all scared and I don't even know why, like this guy is going to be giving us a test, or judging us, or something. I want him to like us, even though I don't like him, with his stupid little teeth and his "Everybody stand up."

We're all standing, and Dr. Meagher tells us, "Stand anywhere you want to." He sees me looking at the door and adds, "Anywhere *in* the room."

Well, it was a good thought.

We're all looking at each other. We're all thinking: *Does everybody know what's going on except me?*

Dr. Meagher sees we're not moving, so he says, gesturing, "Walk around the room, and stop where you're most comfortable."

Despite the fact that this is stupid, we do what he says. I stop near the door, figuring there still might be a chance to make a break for freedom, no matter what he says. Dad walks to the window. Mom stands behind the sofa, with Bryan trying to burrow himself into her side. Wally picks a spot halfway between me and Mom.

I'm sure all this proves something in psychologist-eze, because Dr. Meagher is wearing a self-satisfied smirk.

As if we haven't had enough fun, he says, "OK, now everybody take one step in any direction."

Dad pretty much just shuffles his feet, which I decide to use as my tactic, too. Mom takes one giant step away from Dad, toward Wally, taking Bryan with her. Bryan scales up Mom's body as though she's a jungle gym. Wally moves toward Mom, which takes him away from me, and even I can see the significance of that. Dumb psychologist games. How long did he have to go to psychologist school to learn how to humiliate people?

"Did we do OK?" Mom asks.

"That wasn't a test," Dr. Meagher says, though we all know it was. He can see that she isn't convinced. "You did fine," he assures all of us. "Just fine. Everybody sit back down."

I like sitting better than standing. My knees don't shake so obviously.

"So," Dr. Meagher says, beaming at all of us—if someone with such truly crummy teeth can actually be said to beam, "why are we here?"

I don't say what I'm thinking, which is, *Well, you're obviously here because we're paying you to be here.* We all shuffle our feet some more, or concentrate on settling into our various chairs and sofas, and we definitely avoid making eye contact with Dr. Meagher or with one another, while anyone with any sense at all could see that each of us is desperately thinking, *Call on someone else, not me.*

"Mr. Casselman," Dr. Meagher says. "You've come the farthest to be with us today. Why did you come?"

Dad in his separate chair jerks his chin at Mom, who's leaning into Wally on the sofa, with Bryan in her lap sucking his thumb. Dad says, "*She* said I had to come."

Dr. Meagher raises his eyebrows.

"She said if I was interested in . . ." He hesitates then finishes, ". . . the welfare of the family, I'd be here."

The family is me and Alison, because Bryan is Mom and Wally's child. Dad isn't any more interested in Bryan than he would be in one of those sad-eyed kids you see in those please-adopt-this-child-from-this-Third-World-country commercials. When Dad says "the family," he means me and Alison, and Alison isn't here.

Dr. Meagher looks at me, in the chair next to Dad's. "Anyone else?" he asks, as though Dad had volunteered his answer.

Dr. Meagher might be saying "Anyone else?" but he's looking at me.

There's absolutely no reason I need to be here, so I don't say anything.

Dr. Meagher doesn't say anything either.

Eventually, Mom can't take the pressure. She cracks under the strain of silence and says, "She's not eating enough."

I sigh, but figure I don't need to get sucked into this: Dr. Meagher can see I'm not wasting away.

But he asks anyway. "Susan?"

"I eat," I tell him. I don't think the trembling of my body reveals itself in my voice.

"Do you feel you weigh what you should?" he asks me.

"I weigh more than Connie," I say, even though I know he doesn't know my classmates, "and less than Wakisha. Dr. Bosco is satisfied with my weight." Dr. Bosco is my pediatrician.

"Why do *you* think we're here today?" Dr. Meagher comes out and asks me.

"Same as my father," I say. "*She* made *me* come, too."

My father winks at me.

The session doesn't get much better. Dr. Meagher says things like, "We need to own this situation as a family," and Mom points out things that are wrong with me.

After fifty minutes that seem to take a week to pass, Dr. Meagher finally lets us go. Dad has an appointment to see him again, alone, tomorrow, before he heads back to California.

That Dr. Meagher must think he's pretty good if he thinks Dad has a problem that he can fix in one session.

Mom tries to make an appointment for me the day after that, but I whine about missing rehearsals, and Dr. Meagher is in favor of me having steady, regular things in my life. But before I can celebrate, he says he has Saturday-morning hours. Oh, joy!

He'll continue to see Bryan once a week alone and once with Mom or Wally. Mom and Wally will start coming in as a couple.

I figure the man must be saving up for a nice big Caribbean vacation.

34

Wakisha invites me to a Halloween party and sleepover. My mother calls up Mrs. Carsonne, because she's never met her, and asks her about three hundred questions about the party in particular and maybe a hundred more questions of a more general nature, which are obviously meant to reveal the Carsonnes' views on child-rearing, morality, nutrition, entertainment, and whether there's likely to be intelligent life in outer space.

Apparently Mrs. Carsonne passes the test.

Mortified, I tell myself I'm just lucky Mom didn't demand to speak to Mr. Carsonne also, and Wakisha's younger brother and sister.

My hair has calmed down enough that I don't even have to go as Don King. Instead, I dress up like a girl from the 1950s with a round poodle skirt, white socks, and a ribbon for my ponytail.

Wakisha has a fairy princess costume, complete with sparkles, shimmery wings, and a long blond wig.

Connie comes as a clown, wearing a wig that looks surprisingly like my hair did when I first got my perm, except that this one is rainbow colored. She's got on clown make-up and a rubber nose attached by a string around the back of her head. However, the majority of her outfit seems to come from her father's closet: size-12 high-top sneakers, tee shirt that says BETTER 50 THAN DEAD, a flannel shirt worn upside down, a tie with tiny men playing golf on it, and boxer shorts with yellow smiley faces worn over satin pajama bottoms (I hope not Mr. Miraglia's). Connie also has a very annoying plastic kazoo left over from last Christmas, but I have the feeling that's not going to last the night.

Joanne Tramonto is here wearing a beauty mark and a lot of aluminum foil because she's supposed to be Madonna.

Bertie Dunbar has come in a bunny costume her aunt made for her younger brother last year. She's wearing white knee socks and has her arms wrapped with surgical gauze to hide the fact that the bunny suit's arms and legs are considerably shorter than hers.

Wakisha has also invited two girls I don't know—Vanessa and Sonja—who live on her street. Vanessa doesn't say much but giggles at everything anybody else says. Sonja has a tendency to be bossy, but she does have good ideas. Sonja is dressed in her mother's wedding gown, and Vanessa is wearing a tuxedo. Periodically they link arms and freeze, pretending to be the top of a wedding cake.

The Carsonnes have ordered in pizza, and they must have been popping corn all afternoon. There're enough soft drinks

139

to make us burpy and silly. We have the whole basement to ourselves, except that Wakisha's brother and sister keep sneaking down here, and then they jump out at us, trying to scare us. Wakisha yells, "Ma!" and her mother tells the kids to leave us alone, and ten minutes later they're back.

Wakisha's grandmother, who lives with the Carsonnes, insists that we bob for apples, try to walk with gourds balanced on our heads, and try to eat sugared doughnuts hanging by strings. All of which are more fun than they have any right to be.

From six to seven, we go to the mall, where the stores have people handing out candy to anybody willing to wait in the lines. We hear a few comments about too-old kids, but Sonja answers that looking old is just part of our costumes, that we're really eight-year-olds.

In the mall, I spot Alison in the shoe store, and I'm so glad to see her that I don't even think, *What's the matter with her, trying on shoes when she's got about two dozen pairs in the closet at home?* But then she looks up, and it's just some blond teenager, not Alison at all.

Back at the Carsonnes', we play loud music, eat candy, and try to scare the little kids who come trick-or-treating to the Carsonnes' door.

When we've eaten too much to be able to make it up and down the stairs anymore, Wakisha tells us she's rented two scary movies to keep us up all night. First, she puts on *Psycho*, which—we all agree—isn't all it's cracked up to be. Wakisha's grandmother has told us we'll never again feel safe taking a shower, but how can you be scared when the blood is in black and white? We don't find it the least bit scary, and we start fast-forwarding.

The second movie is about these nasty little creatures that feed on human flesh, but it's more dumb than scary. We give up before the end.

Wakisha starts looking through the cabinet where her family keeps their videotapes, but the only thing we can all agree on is *How the Grinch Stole Christmas*. We watch that, but it's only a half-hour long and afterward Wakisha is back to reading titles from the tapes that her family has recorded. Suddenly she says, "How about the Robert Deitz documentary? That's got some pretty gruesome bits where they show police photos of the bodies."

Real quick, without even looking at me, Connie says, "Everybody's seen that already."

"I haven't," Vanessa says.

Sure. Just about the only thing she's said all evening. I think maybe I'll strangle her.

"You didn't miss much," Connie says.

So, I think, *Connie watched it, too.*

But Bertie says, "No, it's cool. They have this one interview hat Channel Three did, talking with a bunch of prostitutes, fter people saw that there was a pattern but before Deitz was aptured. And it's real spooky because there's this one prosti- ute, she's kind of pretty and she seems sort of nice and all, and then they say that she disappeared later the same night they recorded the interview."

"You mean he killed her that night?" Vanessa asks, like she's got a shiver going up her back.

Bertie shrugs. "He only admitted to the ones they found bodies for. There's a whole bunch who disappeared that nobody knows *what* happened to them."

"Maybe they went away to someplace safer," Vanessa says. Which is sweet, if naive. I decide not to strangle her after all.

"Someplace safer," Joanne scoffs.

"I vote no," Connie says, though nobody's asked, because she's seen that Wakisha is bending over to put the tape in the VCR.

"I second," I say real quick.

Vanessa hesitates, then says, "I third."

"I vote yes," Bertie says.

Joanne says, "It's not like anybody's coming up with any better ideas."

Which brings it to three to three, with Sonja holding the tie-breaking vote.

"Robert Deitz," Sonja says, waving her hand dismissively. "That's not the scariest thing that's ever happened in Port Champlain. Let me tell you . . ." and she launches into a long but well-told goosebump-raising story, which turns out to be a variation on the hook-hand story.

Then Wakisha tells us about some little girl who fell into the foundation hole when Mother of Sorrows was being built and how the concrete was poured on top of her, and sometimes when you're alone in the basement you can hear her scratching at the underside of the floor, trying to get out.

Then Connie tells about this other little girl who appears on foggy nights on Lake Avenue, crying and crying and begging for help, and when you follow her, she leads you straight to Holy Angels cemetery, where she disappears among the tombstones.

At which point Wakisha's mother comes down the stairs, nearly giving every one of us a heart attack.

She shakes her head as we continue to clutch at each other and shriek. "You'd better settle down," she warns us. "Six o'clock is going to come fast."

Luckily, the Carsonnes have two bathrooms, or we'd never all be able to get ready for school tomorrow without getting up at three o'clock in the morning.

I volunteer to take my shower tonight, since that will work out better with my hair, and Wakisha says she'll take one tonight, too, because all the sparkles she's sprayed on her face and arms are beginning to itch.

We need two other girls for a second shift tonight, and they draw doughnut holes to see who it'll be. Sonja and Joanne lose, getting the holes with powdered sugar, though Sonja tries to lick hers off.

Since this is, after all, Wakisha's house, she gets settled faster. I take longer to gather my stuff, and, as I pass by the big bathroom on my way to the smaller one off her parents' bedroom, I hear Wakisha humming to herself and the water running.

Then I hear a very loud scream.

The bathroom door flies open and Wakisha's little brother and sister come tearing out, laughing and running so fast they almost knock me down.

"You little perverts!" I hear Wakisha scream, between gasps for breath. "Ma!"

OK, OK. So, well, maybe *Psycho* is a little bit scary.

35

Rehearsals start pushing quarter of six, until the parking-lot parents complain again. Father Kevin makes sure we get out at five-thirty, but we add Saturday afternoons.

Saturday mornings, I visit the psychologist, which is a waste of my time and Mom and Wally's money. Dr. Meagher tapes our sessions, and I'm sure he plays those tapes for Mom and Wally, even though he swears he doesn't. I tell him—just in case Mom *is* listening—how Mom has made Alison's room into a shrine, how she dusts and vacuums in there, and how she continues to add to Alison's stuffed tiger collection, even though when Alison moved out she left behind what she already had.

"And how do you feel about that?" Dr. Meagher asks. He's *always* asking how I feel about everything.

Telling him my feelings is absolutely the last thing I'd ever want to do. Boy, would he run quick to tell Mom and Wally.

That Susan, he would tell them, *is sometimes relieved Alison went away.* And then they would hate me.

So I answer, "I wish Mom would dust *my* room." A nice girl can say that, joking. I smile, to show I'm joking.

I'm so busy with the play, I sometimes forget that there's an outside world.

The Wednesday before Thanksgiving, there's no rehearsal, and there won't be any again until Monday. There are just too many people who will be away on family vacations. Father Kevin obviously thinks this is very inconsiderate of all the people involved—as though they would have out-of-town relatives just to delay his rehearsal schedule—but even he has to admit it would be useless to have rehearsals with only half the cast members present.

That afternoon, Ms. LaMond suddenly gives me The Look as I'm entering study hall, and I go up to see her. I'm already beginning to feel withdrawal symptoms, because we will *not* be visiting out-of-town relatives and my days will feel empty without Connie, who *will* be away, and without rehearsals.

The last thing in the world I need is Ms. LaMond.

Ms. LaMond asks me, "Did you ever get a chance to tell Alison about that art contest?" she asks.

"Yes," I tell her. "I guess she has three or four really good ideas, and she's been working them all up and trying to decide which is best."

"Oh, I'm so pleased," Ms. LaMond says.

"I forgot to tell you that she asked me to thank you."

"Oh, that's all right," Ms. LaMond assures me.

I go back to my seat and Gina Mack passes me a note that says, "The sister that makes the rest of the world look like dogs?"

I cross out the question mark and change the word "dogs" to "dog food."

Gina nods sympathetically.

36

Three grandmothers and two grandfathers show up for Thanksgiving dinner at our house: Grandma Casselman, who's my father's mother, Grandma and Grandpa Hondorf, who are Wally's parents, and Grandma and Grandpa Walsh, my mother's parents.

I enjoy every single one of them, separately, any other day of the year.

None of them gets along very well with the others.

Also, there is my mother's sister, Kate, and her husband, Nate. They have brought along, uninvited, as they always do, their dog, a fourteen-year-old—and that's people years, not dog years—basset hound, whose name, entirely by coincidence, is Wally.

Nobody gets along at all with Kate, Nate, or Wally.

All the men want to watch football, but all the men have different favorite teams.

All the women want to help in the kitchen, but Mom likes to keep her kitchen to herself.

Wally—the dog, not the stepfather—hangs around the kitchen, constantly underfoot, hoping for scraps. Little does he know that my mother hates dogs and his only chance to get *anything* from her would be to trip her while she's carrying something. Or maybe he does know this, for he has the uncanny ability to choose the most inconvenient place to lie down. Kate and Nate always feed him from the table, which makes Mom crazy, because they'll reach down and hand feed him, then use those same hands to pass the corn or to break the bread apart. Once Wally has eaten all that nice, rich food, he lies down in the middle of the living-room floor, blocking the TV, and passes gas.

Bryan—clever boy that he is—says he won't come out of his room until the football's over because he can't stand to see Grandpa Hondorf, Grandpa Walsh, and Uncle Nate get so excited.

I tell Mom *I'm* going to have an anxiety attack and better stay in *my* room, but she doesn't buy it.

Mom asks me to keep my grandmothers entertained in the living room, but they're certain that my mother needs their help and just won't admit it.

Grandma Casselman slips away from me while I'm busy handing out copies of my school picture to the other relatives. She already has hers, and she wants to make sure Mom has all the lumps out of the mashed potatoes this year.

Once Grandma Casselman's made her break, the other two grandmothers know that there's no holding them back. One year, in a moment of weakness, Mom relented and allowed Grandma Walsh to make the gravy. Now Grandma Walsh is the resident expert on gravy, and she enters the kitchen and starts getting out the supplies she'll need.

Grandma Hondorf has made snide remarks for the last couple years about Mom using Stove Top stuffing, so this year Mom has gone all out and made chestnut stuffing. Now, however, because it's stuffed, the turkey is taking too long to cook. Grandma Hondorf goes into the kitchen to turn on the oven light and watch the turkey cook.

Grandma Walsh, of course, can't make the gravy until the turkey is done, but rather than go back to the living room, she stays in the kitchen and helps Grandma Hondorf watch the turkey.

Meanwhile, the corn and potatoes are just sitting there, getting mushy.

Mom takes the turkey out of the oven and pokes the breast with a knife. She's obviously done this a couple times already, because the turkey has other knife scorings—like it's a tough-guy turkey that's been in street fights.

"I think it's ready," Mom says. "We don't want it to get dry If it isn't done, we can zap the slices in the microwave."

Grandma Hondorf doesn't like microwave ovens. She con siders them new technology and isn't convinced that the really cook food. She starts telling about her neighbor Rose who was sent to the hospital from eating improperly prepared turkey at her brother-in-law's house, and then she got bed sores from careless nurse's aides and had to stay until they cleared up, during which time she caught Legionnaires' disease from the air-conditioning system, and then she died. All from microwaved poultry.

Mom sticks the turkey back in the oven.

Kate doesn't cook. She and Nate eat all their meals out, except breakfast, so she has no advice for my mother. She just hangs around the kitchen, nibbling from the dishes, passing goodies down to Wally. (The dog, not the stepfather.)

Last week Wally (the stepfather, not the dog) said to my mother, "Why do you always subject yourself to this? Why don't we make reservations at a restaurant and eat out? Let somebody else have the aggravation of cooking and cleaning up."

But Mom says Alison might call, since it's Thanksgiving, so she won't leave the house.

Finally everybody agrees the turkey is done.

Both Grandpa Hondorf and Grandpa Walsh consider themselves masters at the art of carving a turkey. To keep feelings from being bruised, we don't allow either one of them to carve. *Wally* carves. And, good as he is with a saw and a piece of wood, he isn't nearly so proficient with an electric knife and a turkey. This is the one thing Grandpa Hondorf and Grandpa Walsh agree on.

We sit down to eat just as the football game goes into overtime. Bryan comes down from his room only after Grandma Casselman bribes him with five dollars. The grandfathers and Uncle Nate refuse to sit in the dining room but stand in the hallway holding their plates so they can see the TV.

The turkey, as Mom predicted, is dry. The mashed potatoes, as Grandma Casselman prepared them, are runny. The gravy Grandma Walsh made is cold. The stuffing Grandma Hondorf insisted on has obnoxious hard bits of chestnut, on which Kate bites down and loses a filling.

Watching the game from the hallway, Nate accidentally drops a gravy-soaked biscuit.

Wally—the dog—who's supposedly here because he's too old and infirm to be left alone at home, dashes across the room faster than any of the quarterbacks could have made it, toenails skittering on the floor, and wolfs down the entire biscuit without chewing. A moment later—just as the football game ends and Grandpa Hondorf says, "Ha!" and Grandpa Walsh pounds his fist on the kitchen counter and Nate shouts, "Idiots!"—Wally upchucks.

Mom jumps to her feet, accidentally tugging on the tablecloth so that the candle tips over, spilling hot wax on the pumpkin bread.

Wally—the stepfather—tries to pick up the candle, but it's still hot and he drops it again, so that this time it lands with a splatter on the white tablecloth.

The grandmothers start arguing about the best way to get wax out of fabric.

Kate's still carrying on about her filling.

Bryan starts to cry and wets his chair—it's hard to say which comes first.

And I just sit there, wishing I was part of Wakisha's family, even with her little brother and sister.

And Alison never does call.

37

The closer we get to the weekend of the performance, the less chance there is to talk to Matt—though I have a hard time convincing Connie of that. But the further along we get, the more there is to do. There are costume fittings, walk-throughs with the scenery, props to get used to—assorted hats and canes and umbrellas, as well as the helium balloons and pompoms. Problems become evident. Like that Mary Amber—Leonora—doesn't have enough time for a costume change between two numbers.

"And meanwhile what am I supposed to do with this baton?" she demands, for the benefit of the prop boy, who wasn't where he was supposed to be.

I have a suggestion, but I politely keep it to myself.

Spencer, who's supposed to be responsible for only the lights, takes the baton.

"The backdrop for the hula dance is never going to be finished in time," the head carpenter warns.

"The fog from the smoke machine makes the dancers' eyes water and they can't see where they're going."

"The scrim keeps getting stuck halfway down."

Problems, problems, problems. I have my own, too. Like every time Matt passes by while Connie is next to me, she gives me a little shove in his direction.

"Stop it," I tell her. "He's going to think I'm spastic."

Or maybe he'll think I'm drunk. Today I fished his ginger ale bottle out of the garbage and drank the two or three drops that were left. Beer again. I'm not impressed with the taste, but I feel very sophisticated. I wonder if he can smell the beer on my breath.

"Talk to him," Connie insists.

"*Tap* those canes!" Mrs. Fallahi calls across the auditorium. "Five, six, seven, eight, *turn*! Shoulders *straight*! Arms *out*! *Turn!* You, in the second row, keep up!"

Lord, is that me?

"Come on, Sibyl," whispers Jeremy, behind me. "I'm following you."

How come I get yelled at for being half a beat off, while Jeremy, who can never remember any of the moves and always watches the people around him, gets away with being two steps behind the rest of us?

"And down and up, and down and up, and smile, smile, smile!"

One of these days, I decide, I really must kill Connie.

Then suddenly I notice Father Kevin and Mrs. Fallahi standing side by side, looking directly at me. Mrs. Fallahi crooks her finger at me. Sure—just when I've gotten used to the idea of being in this play—she's going to throw me out.

Hesitantly I leave the security of the second row and go to the edge of the stage. I lean down.

"Young lady," she says, "you appear to be throwing the entire second row out of synch during this number."

I can't very well deny it. "I'll try harder," I say.

Mrs. Fallahi shakes her head. "I'm going to take you out of this number," she says.

My heart sinks. "Broadway Memories" is not only the flashiest routine in *Love in the Spotlight,* but it's the finale. The full cast is involved. I won't even be on stage to take a bow at the end.

"All right," I manage to say.

Mrs. Fallahi is still shaking her head. "I don't think she understands," she tells Father Kevin.

I suspect I do, but Father Kevin is grinning, which is not like him—to fire someone and be heartless about it.

"We're going to give you a speaking part," Father Kevin says.

"What?" I whisper.

"The girl from Iowa," Father Kevin says. "You'll come on with a sequined gown and a suitcase, run out in front of the curtain and say—"

Matt Burke—I hadn't even noticed he was there—supplies my line: "'Won't anybody show me how to get to Broadway?'"

Father Kevin says, "Then Joe"—that has to be Joe

Delisanti, who's standing next to Matt—"will come out, dressed in a tuxedo, take your hand, and lead you around the walkway."

"Walkway?" I echo.

"It's a crescent-shaped extension," Father Kevin explains, "which will jut out around the orchestra pit . . ." He indicates almost into the front row. "Behind you, the curtain will rise on—"

"The entire cast," Mrs. Fallahi says, "singing 'Broadway Memories.'" She doesn't add, "and dancing in synch."

"Wow," I say.

Matt tells me, "Why don't you go back now to talk to Cindi about your costume?"

"Thank you," I tell them.

I turn around and see Connie looking so pleased that you'd think this was all her idea.

Which, I guess, it was.

Wow, I think again as I head for the room where the costume people are set up. *My chance to glitter.*

38

The performances will be the last weekend before the partial week before Christmas vacation.

Two weeks before *that,* the Mother of Sorrows newspaper, the *Gabriel,* publishes an article about *Love in the Spotlight.* It lists the names of the girls involved, and Connie and I are both in the column that's labeled PERFORMERS rather than the one labeled ALSO, IN THE CHORUS even though all I have is nine words.

Mary Amber DeFranco, of course, gets her picture on the front page.

The day the newspaper comes out, Mr. Rosenblum clips the article about the play and staples it to the current events board, and he gives me a wink when he sees me noticing. Normally he takes down the articles at the end of the day to make room for the next day's news. But he leaves the *Gabriel* article up, and, apparently, it's going to stay up until the perform-ances are over.

Because there are so many Mother of Sorrows girls in-volved, some of the other teachers get excited, too. Miss Beck-with gives us a math worksheet that she's made up especially for the occasion, with questions like: "If there are thirty-seven actors in the *Love in the Spotlight* cast, and there have been forty-six rehearsals lasting two and a half hours and twelve re-hearsals lasting five hours, except that thirteen actors were ab-sent for five of the two-and-a-half-hour rehearsals, and four actors each missed one of the five-hour rehearsals, and one ac-tor who was present every day had to leave a half-hour early every other day, how many man-hours have the actors put into the performance?" The answer, of course, is too many, but I don't say so.

In Italian, Signora Torres teaches us the difference between *bravo* and *brava,* and *bravissimo* and *bravissima.*

In music, somehow Mrs. MacNeely has gotten the words and music for "Broadway Memories." She asks if the per-formers would like to stand in front of the class and run through it once, which we do, though I nearly shock her off the piano stool when I suddenly belt out, maybe a bit louder than is absolutely necessary, "Won't anybody show me how to get to Broadway?"

In study hall, Ms. LaMond tells me that Father Kevin is her nephew and that she's going to be helping out at all three per-formances with the ticket sales, so she'll see me there. She also tells me to break a leg, which—though I know it's a show business term—in my case seems like tempting fate. I go back to my desk and realize it's the first conversation we've had that doesn't involve Alison.

Ha! I think at Alison. And then feel guilty for it.

In film appreciation, we start *A Star Is Born,* which, we're told, has been remade several times and has given rise to many similar though differently named spinoffs. We, of course, watch the 1937 version, in black and white.

39

At rehearsal, they're passing out posters, which we're supposed to put up all around Port Champlain to advertise *Love in the Spotlight.*

I volunteer to bring a batch to Mother of Sorrows, since they're excited about the play already. This way, I won't have to go up to store managers and introduce myself and beg to use up some window space.

Mrs. Miraglia suggests that we stop by at Mother of Sorrows, so I can put the posters in my locker and not have to drag them with me on the bus tomorrow morning. Which is fine—especially since the last couple of mornings it's been snowing—except that my locker is so crowded with junk that I have to clean some of it out before I can get the posters in without scrunching them.

Two of the things I throw out are the envelopes Ms. La-Mond gave me for Alison.

40

There will be three performances: Friday night, Saturday night, and Sunday afternoon.

A couple hours before Thursday night's dress rehearsal, I start wondering again how Connie ever talked me into this.

Friday night, as a whole roomful of girls tries to primp all at once, Connie—who's been asking the same thing every day for the last two weeks—asks me, "Did you invite Matt to the dance yet?"

"Not quite yet," I admit. Why would a gorgeous, sophisticated senior—brave enough to drink beer under the very noses of the faculty of Cardinal O'Gorman—even *consider* going with a freshman like me to a dance put on by nuns? He's been nice to me, but then, he's nice to all the girls.

Connie pinches my arm so hard I squeal.

Nobody seems to notice. A lot of the girls are doing warm-up scales and meditation exercises.

"It's this coming Wednesday," she reminds me.

"I know," I tell her, rubbing my arm.

As soon as I stop, she pinches me again. "Ask him tonight."

"Ow. Stop it." I dodge her, but she shifts to the other arm.

"Ask him tonight," she repeats.

"Stop it," I warn her, "or I'll pinch back."

She gets in another quick pinch but evades mine. "It'd be simpler just to ask him," she points out.

"I know," I say. "I will. I have every intention to."

I think that should make me safe, so I let down my guard, and she pinches me again. "When?" she demands.

"When the time is right," I say.

But just then Matt Burke bangs on the dressing-room door to be heard above the singing, meditating, arguing, and general hysteria that's going on. "Five minutes to curtain positions!" he calls.

I see the manic gleam in Connie's eyes, but I'm not fast enough to clap my hand over her mouth. "Wait!" she calls out to him. She opens the door despite the frantic protests of several of the girls who aren't quite dressed yet, and she shoves me out into the hall, then slams the door shut so that Matt and I are alone in the hall.

Except that we aren't alone.

Sigrid is there, too, her eyes bright, her nostrils flared. She spins gracefully away from Matt and stalks toward the auditorium with the poise of someone who knows she's being watched with admiration.

Good timing, I tell myself. I'm sure Matt is delighted to have had me interrupt their little chat.

"Ah . . ." I say.

Matt looks at his watch.

"It can wait," I tell him.

From behind the closed door, Connie's voice calls out, "No, it can't."

I take Matt's arm, despite his obvious impatience, and pull him one or two steps farther down the hall. If I'm going to humiliate myself, at the very least I can spare myself witnesses. "It's just . . ." I say. "You see, I was wondering . . . Well, Mother of Sorrows is having this kind of, uhm . . ."

"What?" Matt prompts me.

I close my eyes. "Dance." I wait for him to tell me he's busy that day. Then I remember I haven't told him what day the dance is. I open my eyes and see that he is looking at me appraisingly, a different look from any he's ever given me before. "So," he says, sounding pleased with himself, despite the fact that a moment earlier he was breathing heavily. His cheeks are a hectic red, which is not unbecoming.

My language skills deteriorate to preverbal level. "Ah . . ." I say.

"When?" he asks.

I manage to croak out, "Wednesday."

Here it comes.

"All right," he says.

For a second I can't believe what seems to be happening. Then I realize: He was flirting with Sigrid, I deduce, and she turned him down. That would explain the brief instant he looked flustered. His ego is deflated, and he's feeling rejected and vulnerable. Matt Burke, of all people, needs to be reassured he's desirable. Even if it's only someone like me who's doing the desiring.

"Wow," I say.

He grins at me and waggles his eyebrows.

"Thank you," I say. Is it proper etiquette to thank someone for accepting an invitation? What would Miss Manners say? Who cares? Miss Manners isn't going to the Mother of Sorrows freshman dance with Matt Burke.

Matt says, "I got you that role, you know."

I fight the inclination to be silly, to say, "A roll is good, but a muffin is better." Instead, I just say, again, "Thank you."

He leans close, which is disorienting, without my glasses, with him coming suddenly into focus.

Behind him, someone has set up a mirror in the hallway, and—even without my glasses—I get a too-clear look at my face. The make-up people have used thick pancake make-up to give me a ghastly tropical tan and have lacquered my dark hair into position with more hair spray than Wakisha used on it; they've slathered on green eye shadow, thick enough to make us have faces for the back-row audience, we were told. I look down at my toes, but my mind has gone totally blank.

Matt says, "You can thank me properly later."

He has hold of my arm, just my arm. I'm not sure exactly what's lacking that should be there, or what's there that shouldn't be, but his words don't sound playful. They sound businesslike. Maybe I should have made that crack about the muffin after all. I find myself thinking of those stupid analogies they're always giving us on those awful standardized tests: Favor is to reciprocation, as service is to . . . payment, maybe?

Still, I think . . . *Still.* With or without my glasses, he is *so* good looking; he makes my toes cramp from the exertion of trying to keep my feet planted on the ground. *I'm just nervous,* I tell myself. *That's what's causing that little tug of worry.*

Matt pulls me in closer and whispers, "I know someone who can get us fake IDs."

"We don't need IDs to get into the dance," I tell him—not exactly on top of things and trying very hard *not* to be. I tell myself to stop playing dumb. He's obviously a lot more experienced than I am, and I don't want to turn him off. The ego-deflated, vulnerable Matt is gone.

"We'll tell your *parents* we're going to the dance," he explains. "We can go someplace good."

I want to go someplace good. I desperately want to go someplace good. Can I lie convincingly to my parents? Alison could. I try to nudge Alison back out of my thoughts. I am not Alison. But it's hard not to think of how efficiently Alison could lie. And how easily my parents would fall for it. How we all would fall for it.

Matt says, "And, after that . . . my brother has his own apartment."

He wants *me*. Not Sigrid. Not Connie.

Not Alison.

Once again I give Alison a mental shove out of my brain. But in the vacuum that Alison leaves, of all people Dr. Meagher steps in. *How do you feel?* Dr. Meagher's voice asks me. *How do you feel about that?*

Flattered, I tell Dr. Meagher. *Lucky.*

Matt is telling me, "You can show your appreciation to me, and I can show my appreciation to you. We can have a good time."

I pause to sort this out. Has he or hasn't he just indicated to me that both of us would need to be drunk before we could have a good time together?

Stop being so critical, I tell myself. What I need to figure out is how a normal person would react, a person who didn't have Alison for a sister. *How do I feel?*

Well, I tell myself, *I might not be Sigrid or Connie, but I think I resent the implication that I'm THAT bad.*

I test out the feeling.

Oh, yeah: I really *do* resent that.

Girls have begun coming out of the dressing room to take their opening positions, brushing past us, chatting excitedly.

I tell Matt, "I need time to think."

Matt looks dumbfounded, but he recovers quickly. He pulls me in closer yet and kisses me, hard. "A kiss for luck," he says. He adds, suggestively, "For both of us."

A whole cluster of girls exits the dressing room all at once, laughing and talking excitedly. Connie comes out, too, since—obviously—our privacy is gone anyway. Over Matt's shoulder, I see her smile at how close we're standing.

Now that we *are* standing this close, I begin to pay closer attention to his face. What I took for an excited flush on his cheeks is probably something else, I decide, based on the fact that his left cheek is much redder than his right—and that the splotch is roughly palm-shaped.

My mind wanders to some of the movies I've seen in film appreciation, and I wonder, *Do young ladies still slap young gentlemen who have made ungentlemanly suggestions? Sigrid, Sigrid,* I think, *how 1930s.*

So he asked her, too. And since she said no, he decided to spare himself embarrassment and effort and to settle for someone he was sure would say yes. Someone with no choice.

Suddenly the smell of beer on his breath—beer overlaid by Certs—is no longer enticing and exciting. I am *not* Alison, and I figure I'm at least as perceptive as Sigrid, so I say the most difficult thing I've ever had to say, including the "Products of New York State" speech I had to give in front of the assembled fifth grades. I say, "Thanks for getting me the role, Matt, but I'm not that desperate."

Matt looks angry, like he's about to protest, but then he becomes aware of Connie standing behind him, and he's not going to embarrass himself in front of her.

Matt heaves a big sigh. "Gee, I'm sorry, Sibyl," he says. "My parents and I are going out of town then. But I'm sure you'll find someone to take you, and you'll have a super time. Ninety seconds to curtain positions. Catch you later, kiddo."

"Jerk," Connie mutters. She doesn't know what's happened, but she can see something has gone wrong. She can't look at me, which is OK, because I can't look at her. "I think I left my curling iron on," she tells no one in particular, and she disappears back into the dressing room.

Thanks a lot, Connie. I think. *Thanks a lot, Dr. Meagher.* I know for a fact that no other boy will ever again invite me out in my entire life.

I walk backstage, from where I can hear the nervous coughs of the audience. As though they have anything to be nervous about.

Spencer, the lighting manager, is suddenly at my side. "Good luck," he whispers, handing me a hankie. I don't know how he's seen my tears in the half-light. But he's misinterpreted them. He thinks I have stage fright. "Everything'll be fine," he assures me, patting my hand.

"Hsst!" the stage manager hisses. "The house lights just went up again."

"Well, almost everything'll be fine," Spencer says.

And it *does* go pretty well.

At least until the curtain goes up for the opening number.

41

"Broadway/Home town," we sing, the refrain from "Sunshine in May." The words are simple, and the dance movements aren't bad, except that this is the number they built the bleachers for, and there's this one part when we have to step off the bleachers and back up again—eight times in about four seconds: right foot down, left foot down, right foot up, left foot up. During rehearsals, before the bleachers were built, we'd just step forward and back: What could be easier? We've had the bleachers to practice on for five whole rehearsals.

Step number four, going up, my right heel grazes the higher tier.

Step five down, my dance slipper is halfway off my foot; step five up, I put my left foot on the empty portion of the right slipper.

Step six down, I land on my rear end and seriously consider staying there for the rest of the number.

Luckily, I have enough padding—regardless of my mother's fear of anorexia—that I bounce back up before I have time to think about it. I don't even bother to sing the last verse—I just concentrate on where my feet are for the rest of the number, and I manage to get off stage at the right time and without falling into the orchestra pit.

"Great save!" Father Kevin comes backstage to tell me. He and Matt and Mrs. Fallahi are sitting in the orchestra pit, from where they might or might not be able to stop things from going too far wrong.

As I'm waiting in the wings for the next big number, Spencer whispers, "See, that wasn't so bad. You bounced back so fast, nobody in the audience even noticed. But now you're safe. Bad luck couldn't strike you twice."

It sounds reasonable.

Hah!

Mary Amber DeFranco gets rid of her baton on schedule, but she has her bit of bad luck when the curtains open prematurely while she's still waiting for her beloved pom-poms. She has to do all of "High on Me" kind of waving her empty hands at the audience.

And, of course, there's that unfortunate incident when Stan's umbrella gets caught in Gordie's armpit.

But, all in all, things go fairly well. The show is almost over, and I don't have any more dancing, singing, or smiling to do. I'm looking forward to saying my one line, then going home and to bed where I will hide under the covers and never come out till I'm forty-three.

I wait in my turquoise sequined evening gown and take a deep breath. Why a farm girl from Iowa would get off a bus wearing a turquoise sequined evening gown, I don't know, but I haven't asked for fear I'd be put in a dress like Auntie Em wears in *The Wizard of Oz*. This is Connie's older sister's graduation dress, and it's kind of sexy, even given that I'm two bra sizes smaller than Connie's older sister.

Spencer, of all people, blows me a kiss.

I run out in front of the curtain, left hand shading my eyes, right hand clutching my battered suitcase. I scan the audience. Remarkably, considering I'm not wearing my glasses, I catch sight of Mom, Wally, and Bryan in one of the front rows. Maybe it's because Bryan is waving at me.

"Won't anybody show me how to get to Broadway?" I cry.

One second.

Two seconds.

Three seconds.

"Oh!" I say. "Won't anybody show me how to get to Broadway?"

I squint and can make out Father Kevin. In desperate depression, he has his head buried in his arms on the snare drum. Mrs. Fallahi is resting her face in her hands. Matt is wearing an expression of frozen disbelief. He draws his finger across his throat. Maybe it's a technical theater signal for something or other, but it's beyond me.

I step closer to stage right, where Joe is supposed to come from. The stage manager is grimacing. He shakes his head and gives a shrug. Wonderful.

"Oh, dear," I say, and I can tell my voice is on its way out. "Won't *anybody* show me how to get to Broadway?"

"*I'll* take you to Broadway," declares a voice from behind me. Wrong entrance, but what's that between friends? I turn around, and instead of Joe Delisanti in a tux, there's Spencer Pabrinkis in a sweatshirt and jeans. He holds his arm out to me.

For a second I just stare at him, but then I hear the whisper of the dusty velvet curtain rising, so I take his arm and together we walk down the ramp.

I swirl my ankle-length gown, letting the footlights catch on the sequins, and Spencer tugs on his sweatshirt to get it to cover the top of his jeans. In the space of five seconds we go from cowering, desperate kids to grade-A hams. We gesture back to the troupe on stage, we blow kisses to the audience, we take half the finale to make our exit.

As the curtain comes down, I quote from the play, swooning in Spencer's direction, "'Oh, Willard, Willard, won't you take me away from all this?'"

"Well, would you settle for a movie tonight?" Spencer asks—which is *not* how Willard answers Leonora.

"Oh!" I say, snapping out of character. "I'm sorry, I didn't mean—"

The curtain sweeps up for our second bow.

As soon as it's down again, I turn back to Spencer. "I mean, I—"

"Yes," Spencer says, "but will you come?"

"Me?" I say. *Me* who has never been on a date that hasn't been arranged by my best friend and half her family?

"Don't be so down on yourself all the time," he says. "Yes, *you.*"

Which is a whole different approach from Matt's. Let Alison have the kind of boys Alison likes—I'm not Alison.

"If my parents let me," I say.

There's about as good a chance of that as peace in the Middle East.

"They won't let me," I say. Going to a school dance chaperoned by nuns is one thing, but a movie . . .

So I blurt, without bothering to word it out or wait for the right time, "But Mother of Sorrows is having a dance for the freshmen. Would you like to come to that?"

"Yes," he says decisively.

The curtain is going up again. "It's this Wednesday," I tell him while just our feet to our knees is showing.

"Fine," he says.

The curtain goes the rest of the way up, and I spot my family in the audience and hope—now that I've finally got a date—that I was right about them letting me go.

Mom and Wally stand up, still clapping enthusiastically. Other parents join them.

My first play, my first standing ovation. I hope it's a sign of good things to come.

42

When it's all over and Joe is eventually found—in the bathroom, throwing up from stage fright (where else?)—we all go out into the halls, where the audience has to practically trip over us on their way out the door. Everybody tells us what a great job we did, and we don't care that they wouldn't even be here if they weren't, after all, mostly our friends and relatives.

Connie grabs my hands and jumps up and down squealing, saying that I—and Spencer—made the show. I start to tell her what a good job she did as Jasmine Dawn, but she's swept away by a wave of Miraglias.

Spencer and I stand together, hand in sweaty hand. I know we don't have nearly as many people congratulating us as Mary Amber does, but it feels like it.

Two more performances to go, but I know—no matter what happens—that they can't be as bad, or as wonderful, as this one.

My family finally pushes their way through.

Mom hugs me, getting my make-up all over the shoulder of her coat. "I'm so proud of you," she tells me.

Wally says that I should demand a star on my dressing-room door, pointing out that my original role has expanded by a factor of three. I don't know if he really thinks we have individual dressing rooms. I don't tell him that we consider ourselves lucky that they provided separate rooms for boys and girls. You haven't seen anything until you've seen twenty-five chorus girls all trying to wriggle into black tights at the same time. Wally shakes Spencer's hand and says, "Fine job, young man," like Spencer just graduated from medical school.

Bryan tells me that the play was dumb, but that I was OK.

Spencer has a mother, too, who comes at the same time my family is there. She, also, is taken by the idea of her child being a star. She gushes every bit as much as my mother does, and Spencer is as obviously embarrassed, and pleased, as I am.

Seconds after our families leave, Ms. LaMond comes up to tell me that I look stunning in my borrowed gown. "You handled a difficult situation with true class," she tells both of us.

I feel the night can't get any better than this moment . . .

. . . and it doesn't.

"Did I see your family leaving just now?" Ms. LaMond asks.

I don't tell her that they're waiting out in the parking lot for me. I just nod, and she says, "I thought I recognized your mother, but I just caught a glimpse. Was Alison with them, to see her little sister's debut performance?"

"Yes," I say. "She was here just a minute ago." I'm aware of Spencer watching me, because he has clearly seen that my family did not include anybody who could remotely be construed as a sister, but he doesn't say anything. I continue, "Too bad you missed her. She said to tell you the art project is going well."

"I'm so pleased," Ms. LaMond says. I see her attention get diverted to someone beyond me. "Kevin!" she calls, wiggling her fingers in greeting. To me, she says, "I have to congratulate my nephew, excuse me."

Spencer is still watching me, but still not asking anything, still not saying anything.

Somehow the magic has wandered away. I'm aware that I'm an overly made-up fourteen-year-old wearing somebody else's prom gown and that Mary Amber DeFranco still has a crowd around her and I only have Spencer.

"See you tomorrow," I tell him, and head for the dressing room so I can make it out to the parking lot before Ms. LaMond takes it into her head to go out looking for Alison.

43

I decide I'd better hit my parents with the question of whether I can go to the dance while they're still basking in the glow of my success. Besides, if I ask them right away and they say no, I'll have four and a half days to whine and pester.

As soon as I get into the car, I say, "Thanks for coming to the play."

"We wouldn't have missed it," Mom tells me.

"You were great," Wally says.

Bryan says, "Your boobs show too much."

I check, just to make sure—not that there's that much to check. But Bryan's just being a pain. He thinks all women should wear turtleneck sweaters, the way his kindergarten teacher does. I've even heard him ask Grandma Casselman if she knows her top button's undone. And this doesn't even have anything to do with Alison, because he was too young to notice people's clothes back then.

I should have known that if there was anything immodest about my costume, Mom would have complained already. Now she glances back—she knows, but she wants to check, too—and she smiles at me. If she wasn't looking, I'd twist Bryan's ear for destroying my momentum and putting Mom in mind of clothes that reveal too much.

"And thanks for waiting around for me," I say.

"Our pleasure," answers Wally, who's the one doing the driving.

Enough polite banter.

I take a deep breath and jump in. "Uhm, do you remember Spencer?"

Nobody says anything for a few seconds, then Mom asks, "Was that the nightclub owner?"

"No, no," I say. "Not from the play—I mean, *from* the play, but not one of the characters: Spencer, at the end, who saved your daughter from looking like a total moron." I figure it can't hurt to remind them how much we as a family are indebted to him.

"Oh, yes," Mom says. "Spencer."

"Well," I continue, "he and I were thinking,"—Mom, still facing the back, raises her eyebrows quizzically to keep me going—"we were wondering if it'd be all right . . . You see Mother of Sorrows is having this dance . . ."

That does it.

I see Mom shut down completely. She turns around to look out the front windshield. "Susan," she says in that disappointed voice of hers, which is supposed to make me feel guilty for even asking.

"It's just for the freshmen," I say, so she'll realize that there won't be any older kids around and that it'll be a small gathering. I don't come anywhere *near* telling her about Matt's offer.

"Susan," Mom tells me, "you know we think fourteen is too young to start dating."

"But even the nuns don't think fourteen is too young," I protest. "And everybody is going—Connie and Wakisha and even Sharon Rescher-Smith."

Mom just shakes her head, which I guess is better than the old if-everybody-else's-parents-told-them-they-could-jump-off-a-bridge routine, but it leaves me with nothing to argue against.

I backtrack to: "And it isn't a date, it's just a bunch of us at a dance."

"Don't take That Tone with me," Mom says, and I realize I have been, maybe, getting a little bit loud.

Next to me, Bryan puts his hands over his ears, scrunches his eyes shut, and starts rocking back and forth, humming loudly, not a song, just a single, loud note, like a constipated elephant.

Which is a strong indication that even if he was too young to notice people's clothes when Alison was living with us, he hadn't been too young to notice the arguing.

"Bryan," Wally says sharply.

No effect.

Mom gives me a now-see-what-you've-done look. "Bryan," she says, but if Bryan didn't hear Wally, Mom certainly isn't getting through.

Even though we're almost home, Wally pulls over to the side and puts the car in park. He turns around in his seat to face the back. "Bryan." He forces Bryan's hands from his ears.

Bryan's humming becomes louder and more frantic.

"Stop it," Wally commands.

"No more fighting, *no more fighting, NO MORE FIGHT-ING!*" Bryan chants.

"*Bryan.* Nobody's fighting. We're just discussing. Bryan. Everything's all right."

Bryan goes back to humming. Without diminishing the noise level, he finally peeks open his eyes.

Wally and Mom both smile and nod encouragingly. Even I smile at him and give him a friendly little punch on the leg.

He stops humming.

"Do you want to come up here and sit on Mommy's lap?" Mom offers.

Bryan nods.

I unbuckle him and Wally gets out to bring him around the car. Bryan snuggles into Mom's lap and starts sucking his thumb. Wally comes back around to the driver's seat, and I see the look of exasperation on his face as he starts the car, but he doesn't say anything.

"It's only a dance," I repeat.

Mom gives me a sharp look over Bryan's shoulder.

"When is it?" Wally asks.

Mom turns her sharp look to him.

"Wednesday," I tell him. "Seven till eleven. It's the last day of school before Christmas vacation, so I don't have to get up the next day."

Wally glances at Mom.

Mom is looking like she's just realized this is all Wally's fault: If she hadn't allowed him to talk her into letting me join the play, I'd never have met Spencer and I wouldn't now be asking to go to this dance.

But maybe that *isn't* what she's thinking, because she doesn't say any of that. She buries her face in Bryan's hair and says, "We'll drive you there." I'm too shocked to say anything. "We'll pick you up. Or his parents can. We don't want him driving." I don't interrupt to tell her that Spencer's a couple months younger than I am, so he won't be doing his own driving for at least a year and a half. "We don't want you leaving that dance for *any* reason short of the building being on fire, no matter if it's too noisy, or too boring, or if anybody wants to go across the street to Mc-Donalds. You don't leave unless you call us first, and that's just to pick you up early. We don't want to hear anything else."

I nod enthusiastically to everything.

She adds, "*I* get final veto power on what you wear."

I nod, even to that.

"And," Wally says, "if we even suspect that you've misbe-haved, you're grounded until you're our age."

Bryan takes his thumb out of his mouth to say, in the awed voice that the thought of that deserves, "Wow."

44

Saturday night and Sunday afternoon Joe Delisanti shows up on stage when he's supposed to, and there are no major glitches in the performances.

At the cast party Sunday evening, I feel a real sense of loss. No more rehearsals—what will I do with all my spare time? Such a long build-up, and now *Love in the Spotlight* is over. We're all telling each other we must keep in touch—we're writing mushy things on each other's souvenir programs—but we all know it won't last; we'll drift apart. I look around the Cardinal O'Gorman cafeteria, decorated with balloons and streamers for this special occasion, but the place already looks strange. I no longer belong.

The production staff hired someone to videotape the performance, and they're playing the tape on a big screen. It's fun to watch from the audience's perspective rather than from the second row, but the taping was done Saturday night, not Friday. I'm not planning on ordering a copy. I prefer my own memories.

Cast and crew are keeping pretty much separated—as has been the case all along. Spencer hangs out with his friends and I stick with Connie.

My parents are supposed to pick me up at six. When the videotape is over at five-thirty, I go outside anyway to wait on the front steps.

Spencer comes and sits next to me.

We haven't seen much of each other in the past two days, and he hasn't said anything about the lies he heard me telling Ms. LaMond about Alison. I *have* told him that my parents OK'd the dance, and I *think* he was pleased. Maybe he's wondering if I lied about that, too. It's awful once you become aware of lies—you don't know what to believe. I'm wondering now if he's about to back out, if I won't see him any more than I'll see the other kids from other schools or the Mother of Sorrows upperclassmen.

He says, "Do I need to borrow Joe's tux, or is a sports jacket OK?" which must mean he's still planning on going to the dance. Joe is about a foot and a half taller than Spencer and must outweigh him by about thirty pounds.

"A sports jacket will be fine," I tell him. "I hope you haven't been counting on my wearing Connie's sister's gown." While my mother has no problem with it as a *costume,* I know without asking she'd never let me wear it out in real life.

"Well, you *do* look nice in it," Spencer tells me. "But, then you look nice in your Bugs Bunny sweater, too."

Just then the front door opens, and Connie and Joe Delisanti come out. Connie blows me a kiss as they head for Joe's parents' car, which is already packed with Delisanti siblings.

Matt comes out next, with Mary Amber DeFranco clinging to his arm and squealing from the cold. "Well, we're hitting the road," Matt says. "You kids need a ride? Super show."

Kids? I think.

He just wants to make sure I notice who he's with so that I realize he was just nice to me out of pity.

Spencer and I watch Matt and Mary Amber cross the street and get into Matt's car.

"Mary Amber's a lot prettier than I am," I say as they drive off.

Spencer smiles. "She would never have held her own on stage like you did."

"But she *is* prettier," I insist.

When Spencer doesn't answer, I turn and look at him.

"Well, yes," he says—I'd never again have believed anything he said if he hadn't admitted it—"I guess she is." And then he leans over and gives me my first, honest-to-goodness kiss.

We talk, sitting on the stairs, with the cold seeping into our buns, about the dance, about Mother of Sorrows School and Cardinal O'Gorman School, and about what movies we'd like to see *if* my mother wouldn't get hysterical at the mention of it. The one subject Spencer and I don't talk about is Alison.

Eventually I see that it's almost six-thirty and there is still no sign of my parents. I make a mental note to yell at Mom as much as she yelled at me that time Father Kevin kept us late, except that I'm too cold to care to work it out.

"I think I'd better call home," I say.

Spencer, who's been too polite to leave me, nods enthusiastically.

Except that somehow, while we've had our backs to the building, everyone has gone, and the door is locked.

"Great," I mutter.

Spencer, who has no gloves *and* no pockets, has his hands shoved up his sleeves. "I live four blocks that way," he says, nodding in the opposite direction from my house. "You can come with me and call your parents from there."

"I live about two miles this way," I tell him. Four blocks sounds a lot better than two miles, but my parents are likely to eventually realize that they've forgotten me. If they come here and don't find me either right here or on a direct route home, Mom is likely to lock me in my room for at least the next five years.

"How about if you go to your house," I suggest, "and you call my parents and tell them I'm on my way?"

"I'll come with you," he insists, which is a relief. It's only six-thirty, but in December that means it's as dark as night. Not that this is a bad neighborhood, but still . . .

At first we continue talking as we walk, but then we get so cold our teeth start to chatter. The sidewalks are mostly, but not always, shoveled, and we're both wearing just sneakers on our feet. My jacket is the black leather one that I saved up for with my allowance and the chocolate money. I learn that leather doesn't make good insulation from the cold. I try to get Spencer to put on my mittens, at least for a little while, but he says if he's going to die on the street of exposure, he'd rather not be wearing Tweety Bird mittens when his body is found.

We watch the cars that pass us, but there's no sign of Wally's pickup or Mom's station wagon.

It takes us between twenty minutes and a half-hour to get to our street. We turn the corner, and there's a police car in our driveway.

Oh, no, I think, *not again.*

Just like the bad old days with Alison.

45

Spencer sees the police car in the driveway and asks, "Anybody you know?"

There's no way for him to guess that's our driveway. He's asking if I know the neighbor whose house the police are parked in front of. He can't realize that I *do* recognize the car. Not everybody can identify a police officer by the number on her car. But Officer Susan Howitt used to be practically a regular at our house. For a while, we saw more of her than of Alison.

Out of the corner of my eye, I'm aware of Spencer looking at me. I realize I've stopped walking; I realize I haven't yet answered him. But, for the moment, the moving parts of my body—like my feet and my mouth—don't seem to be working. My very first thought was, as so often before, *What has she done now?* But in reality I realize there's a very good chance that she hasn't done anything in a long time.

Spencer must be sensing that something's wrong, though he probably hasn't guessed what, when our front door crashes open and Wally runs out. He doesn't have a coat, and he's heading for his pickup. My guess is that he's just remembered that he's nearly an hour late to pick me up. The image of how frantic he'll be to find Cardinal O'Gorman all locked up and me not there—the image of him cruising the streets, looking for Alison and me the time we went looking for our father—unglues my mouth.

"Wally!" I call.

He doesn't hear and is already halfway into the truck.

Up until this point, I don't think Spencer recognized him. Now he calls, in that big, booming voice teenage boys can make, "Mr. Casselman!" because I've never mentioned that Wally is my stepfather and that he's Mr. Hondorf.

Wally turns anyway and finally spots us. Despite the cold, he looks ready to melt at the sight of me. He manages a few steps in our direction, but his knees are obviously wobbly, and we meet him at the foot of the driveway.

I suddenly notice that Spencer has taken hold of my arm—*my* knees must look wobbly, too.

"Oh, Susan," Wally says, "I'm so sorry. We didn't realize the time—"

"Is it Alison?" I ask. Of course it's Alison. Why else has Officer Howitt ever been here?

"Yes," Wally says. "No." It had seemed a simple enough question. "Yes," he settles on, "but not the way you mean.

They haven't found her. Come inside—you must be freezing."
He extends the invitation to Spencer, too, by touching his
arm, by asking him—he without a jacket—"Don't you have
any gloves?"

In the living room, Officer Howitt is standing, in that
stiff, military way she has, looking at the pictures on the
mantel, pictures of Alison, and Bryan, and me. She has her
hands behind her back—maybe she's so used to working
with criminals that she wants to make sure nobody could suspect her of planning to grab something and stuff it in her
pocket.

She's standing in front of my favorite picture. A lot of the
others are formal school and baby pictures, but this was a
snapshot that came out so well that Mom and Wally had it en-
larged and framed.

It's all three of us the August between fifth and sixth grades
for me, between tenth and eleventh for Alison. Four years difference in our ages, five in school grades, because Alison was
always smarter than me. Bryan, of course, is a baby. The scene
is our back yard, and the camera is focused in on us, the trees
looking more indistinct and parklike than in real life. Also
better than real life, we look like an incredibly happy, friendly,
nice family. Alison and I are sitting on the grass, Bryan is in
my lap. Alison is laughing, her head thrown back, her golden
hair caught by a breeze so that she looks like a model. Since I'm
only eleven, I look like a little kid, and for a little kid I look
cute. This was before I got braces, which I wore in seventh

and eighth grades and had to learn how to smile with my mouth closed, which I know I still haven't gotten over. I'm propping Bryan up, and he's got his eyes closed, his mouth shaped in a perfect O, so that he looks like a tiny singing angel. There's absolutely nothing in the picture to indicate that two months later—on her sixteenth birthday—Alison would drop out of school and one month after that would disappear entirely.

Officer Howitt turns from the picture as we enter the room, although with her police training I should hope she was aware of our coming into the house.

She tells all of us, "Mrs. Hondorf went to check on Bryan." To me in particular she says, "Hi, Susie. You're looking very grown up." Then she glances at Spencer.

I wonder if she means that I'm acting too grown up by having a boy with me, that I'm acting like Alison. Or is she just looking at Spencer to be polite, to not ignore him? Does she mean I look grown up compared to the picture? "Susie" doesn't sound very grown up. Officer Howitt is absolutely the only person who calls me that. Is she trying to keep me a little kid, or is it just strange for her to say "Susan" since that's her own name?

Wally says, "This is Spencer, who worked on the play with Susan and was good enough to walk her home when we didn't show up."

Officer Howitt shakes his hand. "I can drive you to your house shortly," she offers.

Spencer says, "Give me a few minutes to weigh the excitement of riding in a police car against the likelihood of my mother having a heart attack if she sees me in one."

Officer Howitt gives a little laugh, then glances at Wally, a question in her expression.

"Susan," Wally says, "can you sit down for a minute?"

"Is this something that I need to sit down for?" I ask.

"No," Wally says, at the same time Officer Howitt says, "Not necessarily," but I sit down anyway. Spencer sits next to me on the couch. My legs, especially my thighs, are all prickly from coming in out of the cold.

Mom is just coming up the stairs, which means Bryan is in the basement playroom, which is a relief. I realize I've been assuming he was up in his room, that he'd been put to bed after a bad shock or something.

"What's going on?" I ask before we can be sidetracked by Mom asking how Wally got me home so fast or what Spencer is doing here. "*Is* it something to do with Alison?"

Mom sits down on the other side of me and takes my hand. "Robert Deitz has died," she says.

"So?" I say. I fight the sense of relief, but still I say, "Good." Surely there's more to it than this, or everybody wouldn't be looking so somber about the death of a man who'd killed twelve women and maybe up to seven more. "Did he say something about Alison before he died?" I ask.

Mom says, "He died very suddenly."

"A massive stroke late this afternoon," Officer Howitt adds.

"Nobody saw it coming, and he didn't have time to say anything."

My first thought is that it isn't fair, that after killing so many people Robert Deitz should have such a quick and painless death.

Then the significance sinks in: a dead man has lost the chance to admit to any more crimes. He can't say, finally, whether he killed Alison—and, if he did, what he did with her body. Although I'd been telling myself for the past year and a half that I'd probably never know for sure what happened to my sister, I suddenly realize that I'd been lying to myself: in my heart, I always expected to find out eventually.

Now, for the first time, I really believe I won't.

Unless Alison turns up alive and well, arriving at our house and announcing, "Hello! I've been living in Colorado and decided to let bygones be bygones."

Or unless someone finds the body—which, after three years, must be awfully well hidden.

And that's *certainly* not fair.

46

Wally ends up driving Spencer home rather than subject Mrs. Pabrinkis to undue heart strain by sending him home in Officer Howitt's squad car.

Mom stays at our house to call Dad in California before he hears about Robert Deitz's death on the news.

Spencer sits in the pickup scrunched between us, holding my hand, which Wally probably notices but doesn't say anything about. It's hard for me to guess how much sense Spencer has been able to make of all this.

That Alison is gone and we don't know where, he has to have caught. And that—despite our most fervent wishes—we are presuming she is one of Robert Deitz's victims. What's missing are the details.

Like how Mom blames Abe Lincoln High and the friends Alison made there, though there are strong signs that Alison started running wild that summer between grammar school and high school.

The thirteen-year-olds she had graduated with were having mixed parties. Though Alison, having skipped third grade, was only twelve, apparently she was one of the ones who fell most enthusiastically into making out. She started lying about where she was going and who she'd be with.

Once in high school, she liked to hang around with the junior and senior boys.

And—apparently—they liked to hang around with her.

Her honor-roll grades disappeared. For the first time, report cards came home with negative comments regarding incomplete work, talking back, and disruptive behavior. She started cutting classes or skipping school entirely, and in June—when Mom was taking her school clothes out of her dresser drawers to put away for the summer—Mom found a box of condoms.

Alison insisted that someone had given them to her as a joke, but the lying concerning her whereabouts continued. She started coming home later and later and answering "You can't make me" when she was told she was grounded. She wouldn't even use her real name anymore, but called herself Aly Walsh, as though to distance herself from Mom and Wally. Mom called the police to our house on two occasions when Alison stormed out of the house angry and didn't come home all night long.

In her sophomore year, Alison was arrested, twice, for shoplifting.

By her junior year, Mom and Wally were convinced she was using drugs—not because they ever caught her at it but because she kept stealing money, a substantial amount of it, and because her shoplifting escalated from clothes to electronic gadgets, and because, just after her sixteenth birthday, she offered sex for money to a man who turned out to be an undercover police officer.

A court date was set, but before we ever got there, Alison moved a bunch of her stuff—and a bunch of ours—out of the house, and we never saw her again.

And then the newspaper started printing articles about young women—the kind of young women who offered sex for money—disappearing or being killed.

All that is what I need to tell Spencer, and though Wally certainly knows the details at least as well as I do, I can't say them in front of him. I'll have to call Spencer tonight.

We pull up in front of the Pabrinkis house after a long, silent ride.

"Thanks for the ride," Spencer tells Wally.

"Thanks for seeing my daughter home," Wally answers. "Do you want me to come in and explain to your family why you're late?"

Spencer gives a dismissive wave. "My mother won't have noticed. I mean,"—he remembers we're the family with the missing daughter—"she'll assume the cast party went on longer than we thought."

A normal reaction, for a normal family.

Spencer looks at me and asks, "Will I still see you Wednesday, for the dance?"

"I don't know," I tell him, unwilling to make any decisions at this moment.

"I don't see why not," Wally answers for me.

He and I go home for a very quiet supper, and a very subdued evening, and a very early bed.

What's different? I ask myself. We've learned nothing new. Nothing's changed.

But everything has.

47

On Wednesday, I'm still not sure I'm going to the dance. I'm certainly not in the mood for it, but everybody—Mom, Wally, Spencer, and Connie—seems to be assuming I'll go.

I've gotten a dress to wear—not through any action on my part, but because Robin Liccardi has suggested we trade the dresses we wore to the eighth-grade formal. Mine is ruffled and flowered. Hers is black with an overlay of black lace—very classy and, to my mind, the better deal. But she figures too many people have seen her in it.

"Robin," I tell her, "we graduated from the same school. Everybody who's seen yours has seen mine."

But she figures the dresses will somehow be magically transformed or that nobody will recognize them if they're on different people.

By six o'clock, after an early dinner, I'm still thinking that I really need to get up the energy to call Spencer and cancel. But

Wally won't let me in the kitchen to help with the dishes; he tells me to go upstairs and get ready.

I point out that Robin's dress—though clean—needs to be pressed, and there isn't time to do that *and* fix my hair and put on my make-up, and in any case I don't have black shoes and I certainly can't wear brown with a totally black dress, and sneakers would be even worse, so I'm just going to call Spencer and call this all off.

At which point Mom tells Bryan to go ahead and watch TV: she needs to help me.

The next thing I know, she's dragging me upstairs and telling me to fix myself up. She whips out the ironing board and gets the black dress looking crisp and new by the time I've washed my face. As I'm putting on my make-up, she comes in with a pair of her own black shoes, but they're too big.

"I'll be back in a minute," she says, and I figure she's going to stuff something into the toes, which will never work, but she comes back with a pair from Alison's closet, the first thing to come out of Alison's room since the sweatshirt that was loaned to the police for the benefit of the tracking dogs.

"I can't wear those," I say.

"Why not?" Mom asks, obviously fighting to meet my eyes.

No reason. No reason I can think of.

The shoes are dusty, but they fit, and Wally whisks them away to polish them.

Somehow or other, at a quarter to seven I'm ready, and Spencer shows up at the door.

"Who's driving?" Mom asks, her voice only slightly shivery. "Me or your mother?"

"I've brought my chauffeur and limo," Spencer says.

We look out the window and see a pickup truck that's in worse shape than Wally's. The chauffeur turns out to be Spencer's cousin, Andy, whom I met after Saturday's performance. Andy is eighteen, and I figure there's no way my parents are going to let me go with an eighteen-year-old driver they don't know. But he's wearing a black suit—actually his uniform from his job as a waiter at a Chinese restaurant—and what turns out to be his father's old Marine Corps dress cap. He kisses my mother's hand, salutes Wally, and bows for me to precede him down the front step. Then he runs ahead of me to open the pickup's door.

And somehow Mom and Wally are letting all this happen.

"I hope you're paying him well," Mom tells Spencer with a laugh.

Andy gives a wicked grin that indicates Spencer is.

Spencer gets in through the driver's door so that he rather than I takes the cramped middle position.

"Where to, sir and lady?" Andy asks.

I can't get into the mood. I shrug, not feeling like part of this game. Mom and Wally are waving from the front door, and I wave back, halfheartedly.

"The ball?" Spencer suggests.

I shrug again.

"The ball," Spencer tells Andy.

Andy pulls the truck out of the driveway. When we're halfway down the street, I find that there are tears running down my cheeks. I try to keep my face to the window, but Spencer sees anyway.

"What's the matter?" he asks frantically.

I've been so discreet that Andy has seen, too. He punches Spencer in the arm. "What did you *do*?" he demands of Spencer.

I'm not so far gone that I can't at least defend my date. "Nothing," I assure Andy.

Spencer tells his cousin, "Sibyl and her family just heard some bad news about her sister."

I've explained everything to Spencer, but he obviously hasn't blabbed to Andy, who just says, "Oh" like he's kind of curious but doesn't want to appear nosy. Then Andy asks me, "Don't you want to go to the dance?"

"No," I tell both of them.

Spencer pulls the handkerchief out of his pocket, which is a good thing because I can't find a tissue in my purse. "Do you want to go home?" he offers.

"No," I answer.

There are a few long moments of silence.

Finally Andy—he *is*, after all, the driver—asks, "Where *do* you want to go?"

Without having thought of it—certainly without planning—I blurt out, "The funeral home."

Andy takes off his hat and beats Spencer with it. "Her sister just *died* and you expect her to go to a *dance* with you?"

"No," Spencer says, trying to protect himself from the blows but unsure what to say.

"My sister's not at the funeral home," I say. "Robert Deitz is."

Andy stops beating Spencer. "You want to go to the funeral parlor to see Robert Deitz?" he asks incredulously.

"Yes," I say.

Andy smacks Spencer one more time with the hat—probably for dating a demented girl—but then he asks, "How do we even know where he's laid out?"

"Broman and Fass," I answer. It was in the paper.

With a sigh, Andy shakes his head, but he signals for a left turn.

Before the evening is over, I better let Spencer know it's OK for him to tell Andy about Alison, because—judging by the look on Andy's face—he isn't going to give Spencer any other choice.

48

We have to stop at a gas station phone booth to look up the address of Broman and Fass, but Andy finds the place without any trouble.

Andy says no way is he going to crash somebody's funeral, and he'll wait in the truck.

Spencer comes in with me.

We get in the main doors, but then we see that we're in trouble. There are four rooms off this hallway, each with a sign so that people will know where the dead person they're looking for is. Robert Deitz's name is over the first door on the right—no problem so far. Except someone standing there. He's obviously a guard, despite the conservative charcoal gray suit, and he's intent on letting in family members only and keeping out the curious public.

Even now this man—whether an employee of the funeral home or the family—is arguing with a man and a woman who have brought a camera and are wearing plastic name tags that say PORT CHAMPLAIN TIMES. "Show a little respect for the man's mother, will you?" the guard says. "How's it going to benefit the public for you to ask her what she's feeling?"

I can't hear what the newspaper people are answering, but whatever it is, it must not fully capture the interest of the guard. He glances up and sees us.

And waves for us to go on into the room.

I move without stopping to think, and Spencer, holding onto my arm, moves with me.

It must be our clothes, I figure. Spencer's navy blue jacket and my dress borrowed from Robin are both proper funeral home attire. But then I catch a glimpse of my tear-streaked face in the mirror over the guest book and realize the guard assumed we were family.

The room is large, but it's practically empty. I've been to funerals before, several times, having three sets of elderly great aunts and uncles. Those have been large gatherings, usually noisy, usually involving a lot of milling about and catching up with relatives only seen at funerals and weddings, and—in the case of the Hondorfs—usually including Wally's cousin Lydia slipping Tupperware catalogs into the purses of the other women.

This is nothing like that. There are about ten people, all sitting in a row. Silent. I try not to look at them, but they're all looking at us.

From the side of his mouth, Spencer whispers to me, "Do you want to go closer?"

Which is euphemistic for, Do you want to go right up to the body?

"Yes," I whisper back.

There's a kneeler in front of the casket, but I certainly have no intention of praying for Robert Deitz. *Life,* I think, *is a series of random accidents. Robert Deitz is a random accident.* I stand there, looking down at his face. I'm aware of Spencer next to me, and I can tell by the angle of his head that he's staring at the brass fittings of the casket rather than at the body. But I'm looking directly at Deitz's face. I'm thinking, *This is the man who probably killed my sister.*

Some of the victims had been raped, some not. He admitted to having sex with one woman after she was dead.

Did Alison know about him? I wonder. She disappeared before the newspapers started making a big deal about a serial killer. Did Deitz kill her quickly, before she had a chance to see it coming? Did he say, "Here, get in my car," and then suddenly pull out a knife or a club from behind his back? Or did he pay her to have sex with him first? That's something else he admitted to doing occasionally. Was he creepy all along so that she was afraid of him, or did he pretend to be nice?

He doesn't look scuzzy and demented. In the photos from the newspaper and the evening news, with his loose-fitting prison shirt and his arms shackled, he looked like a killer. Now he looks like a department store mannequin. Who may or may not have been the only person to know what happened to my sister.

I hate him, and all in all I'm glad he's dead, but I'm certainly incapable of some grand gesture like spitting in his face or tipping over his coffin or grabbing him by the lapels of his suit and screaming, "Where is she?"

I'm only aware that I've begun crying again when Spencer tugs on my arm and begins to pull me away. I start to sob uncontrollably.

A woman stands from that silent row of mourners. By her age I guess her to be Robert Deitz's mother.

What kind of mother raises a serial killer?

I want to blame her, since there's nothing I can say to Deitz. But she comes up to me. She doesn't say a word; she doesn't smile or frown or give any indication what she's thinking. She just lays her hand on my arm. And then she returns to her chair.

Spencer leads me out of there, past the well-dressed guard at the door, out the main door. He doesn't bring me to Andy's truck, but sits me down on the waist-level wall that surrounds the parking lot, away from the lights, giving me a chance to pull myself together.

"Life is a series of random accidents," I tell him.

He doesn't look any more convinced than Rosenblum did.

"We fought," I say then, something I never told any of them—not my parents, not the police, not the psychologist, not even Connie. "They think she's the bad girl, because of the things she did." I can barely speak; I know my voice is a whisper. "But I'm the bad girl because *I'm* the one who made her leave."

Spencer squeezes my hand, and I tell the rest of it.

"I caught her in my room, holding onto the money I'd gotten as birthday presents from my aunts and uncles."

I rub my eyes, mascara and all, to stop the tears, to wipe out the picture of me slapping her and the surprised look on her face. I fight not to hear the hateful things I called her nor the way she answered, "Who needs any of you?" as she threw the money at me and stalked out the door.

I locked myself in the room in case she changed her mind. I heard her throwing things around in her own room, and then downstairs, and then the front door slammed.

We never found out where she went. We never saw her again.

Softly, Spencer says, "My God, Sibyl, you can't blame yourself."

No, I think. No, that's true.

I could blame any one of my three parents. I could blame Dad, who I know already blames himself, thinking Alison became boy crazy to prove to herself and the world that she wasn't gay like her father. Then there's Mom, who also blames herself, thinking that if she hadn't divorced Dad, Alison might not have run wild. I've heard Wally blame himself, sometimes for being too easy and letting her get away with too much for too long, and other times for coming down too hard on her.

Probably Grandma Casselman, Grandma and Grandpa Walsh, and Grandma and Grandpa Hondorf feel guilty for some reasons of their own.

Or I could blame Robert Deitz's mother.

Or I could blame Alison, who made her own decisions.

Or maybe it's time to let go of blaming.

Funeral parlors are a place for letting go. Going to the funeral parlor for Robert Deitz is not the same as going for Alison. But it's a beginning.

Funeral parlors are for saying good-bye.

If I can get used to my hair, and to singing and dancing, and to going out with a boy, I can get used to Alison being dead.

I get a mental picture of Dr. Meagher, stupid little teeth and all. *Not now,* I tell him, remembering how his "How do you feel?" routine ruined things with Matt Burke, and even though that was the right choice and everything worked out, I'm busy right now. But Dr. Meagher's voice says: "Take one step in any direction."

One step, I think.

In any direction.

I decide to tell Ms. LaMond what really happened. It will be hard, I know. "Ms. LaMond," I will say when school resumes after Christmas vacation. "I need to tell you something about Alison."

I will say good-bye to Alison.

I will stop feeling guilty that she is gone, and I will stop feeling relieved that she is gone, and I will stop feeling guilty that I feel relieved.

It is time to let go and move on without her.

I will step away from Alison.

Spencer must have grabbed a handful of tissues from Broman and Fass, for he pulls a wad of them from his pocket and starts dabbing at my face. He melts a bit of snow in his hand to moisten the tissue to remove the streaks of mascara.

I use his hanky to blow my nose, noisily.

Finally he asks me, "Do you want to go home?"

"Do I look that bad that I *have* to go home?" I ask.

"You look beautiful," he says—which would have been an exaggeration even at the beginning of this evening.

I let it slide. I tell him, "I want your chauffeur to take us to the ball."

And he does.